The Whistle Blower
A Wing and a Prayer Mystery

New Creation Publishing

Many thanks to Cozy Mystery Author Sarah Hualde for helping me name this series!

Chapter 1

"Mama, Mama, Mama!" Joanna cried from her blanket on the grass.

"What, honey?" Sandra tried not to sound annoyed.

Joanna pointed at the field and began to chant, "Peter! Peter! Peter!" It appeared the coach had put Peter back into the game. At six years old, Joanna worshiped her big brother. Sandra thought probably this wouldn't last forever. She pulled her sunglasses down out of her hair and onto her eyes so she could watch the game without squinting.

Sandra had been sitting there in her folding chair for quite some time, but hadn't really had a chance yet to watch the game. She'd had her hands full keeping Joanna in sight and keeping baby Sammy from screaming.

But now Peter was back on the field, so now she wanted to focus.

A child on the home team, a portly youngster who seemed far too enormous to be in middle school, flattened one of Plainfield's strikers.

The crowd behind her blew up. "How can you not see that?" one mom screamed. "Blow the whistle!" screamed another.

The Whistle Blower

Sandra looked at the referee to see how he was handling such unsolicited feedback and was alarmed to see that he appeared to be at least a hundred years old. *Well, good then, maybe he doesn't hear well.*

The play was long over, but the Plainfield coach was still screaming at the ref. Sandra was embarrassed. It was only their first game of the season, but they'd had several practices, and Sandra knew that Peter really liked his coach. She didn't look forward to trying to explain to her ten-year-old why his coach was swearing at the referee during a middle school soccer game.

Just when she thought he'd calmed down, there was another scuffle at the eighteen, and the Plainfield coach, as well as the Plainfield parents, once again disagreed with how the referee pronounced judgment.

Sandra put her head in her hands.

"Why is everybody so mad, Mama?" Joanna asked, reasonably.

"Not sure, honey," Sandra said quietly.

Peter got the ball. Sandra held her breath. He looked so little out there, a fifth-grade-David amidst a battlefield full of Goliaths. Peter dribbled the ball toward the goal, and then it happened. One of the Philistines came for him. And flattened him like a bug.

There was no whistle. The crowd behind her erupted again. Peter started to cry. Sandra stood up. Her first instinct was to run straight out onto the field and comfort her baby, but he wasn't her baby anymore. Not really. The coach certainly wasn't extending that type of compassion to her eldest.

"Come on, Pete, walk it off," he said.

She knew that Peter didn't like it when people called him Pete. But he did pick himself up and hobble toward the bench. Sandra couldn't help herself from going to check on him, but she did manage to restrain herself from cutting across the field. It wasn't lost on her that no parent did that—ever.

"Come on, Joanna, we're going for a walk."

"Is Peter okay, Mama?"

"Yes, I'm sure he's fine. Let's go."

"Did the angels protect him?"

"Yes, I'm sure they did. Let's go." Her patience tank was running low.

Finally, Joanna stood up and took her hand.

She tried to push the stroller with one hand, but the grass made this difficult. She wished, not for the first time, that they'd sprung for one of those fancy jogging strollers. "I'm going to need both hands," she said, wresting her hand free of her daughter's sweaty clutch. "Just stay with me." Even with both hands, progress was slow. They crept down the touchline and then rounded the corner to travel the goal line. As they did, Sandra sneaked a look at the ancient ref. He didn't look so good. Was something wrong, or was he just too old for this gig?

Before she'd even finished the thought, the official wobbled a little and then his tall, lanky frame crumpled to the ground.

Everything stopped. Joanna stopped walking. The coaches stopped screaming. The other, much younger, ref stopped and stared at his partner. The crowd fell silent. The kids stopped moving and most of them knelt to one knee, something they were trained to do when a player was injured. The ball rolled to a stop in the grass. Sandra looked around to find the closest adult and then realized she was it. *Looks like I'm going to run out onto the field after all.*

"Stay here, honey. Stay right with Sammy." She put her daughter's small hand on the stroller handle, in the probably vain hope that this would tether her there.

Sandra was only twenty feet away from the fallen official, and it didn't take long to reach him. His face was red, he was gasping for air, and he reached up for her as she knelt beside him. She took his wrinkly hand into her own.

"You've got to … stop them … stop them …" he forced out.

"Stop who?" she said, alarmed.

"White," he said, and then closed his eyes.

Many had followed her lead. The field was filling with grown-ups. As Sandra felt for a pulse, another woman touched her on the shoulder. "I'm a nurse. Let me help him."

Sandra moved out of the way, grateful that there was someone more qualified. As she headed back toward her children standing on the goal line, the other referee grabbed her by the arm, not nearly as gently as she would have preferred, if given a say.

"What did he say to you?"

She yanked her arm away. "Nothing! Do you mind?" And she walked away, toward her family, wondering why she'd just lied to a soccer ref.

Chapter 2

"Mom, I don't want to stop at the store," Peter whined. "I'm so thirsty." When she didn't respond to that, he added, "and hungry."

"Well, if you want to eat anything—ever—we need to stop at the grocery store."

"We have food at home!"

"No, actually, we don't, because you consume about six thousand calories per day. Don't worry, it'll be a quick stop."

"You always say that, and it's never quick."

She yanked the rearview mirror down toward her face so she could look her eldest in the eye. "Did you just sass me? That sounded a little too close to sass."

He looked down, ashamed.

"Yeah, that's what I thought."

It wasn't that Peter didn't have a point. Stopping at the grocery store with three children was a giant pain in the rear, but it was also a necessary evil. Their father had meetings and wouldn't be home till late, so if they were going to eat, they had to buy food.

She pulled into the parking lot of the mega-grocery, dismayed to see that everyone else in the state of Maine had also decided to shop at this exact moment. It took her ten minutes to get her three children out of the minivan, the shopping cart disinfected, and her youngest strapped into said shopping cart. Then she noticed Peter was still in his cleats. "Peter!" she snapped. "You can't wear those into the store!" Another five minutes passed as Peter located and changed into his flip-flops. It started to rain. She was grateful it had waited until after the soccer game, but she also wished it could have waited until they got home.

They entered the store, and Sandra shook the rain out of her hair. "Okay, Peter and Joanna, you can each pick out one healthy treat."

"If it's healthy, it's not a treat," Peter mumbled.

"Fine, then don't get a treat. You can eat Brussels sprouts."

"Raspberries?" he said, his voice tinged with hope.

"Sure. That sounds delicious," Sandra said as she sifted through the avocados.

They filled the cart. It looked like a lot, but Sandra knew it would only last a few days with Peter around.

After twenty minutes in the checkout line, Sandra was able to purchase her wares. Then it was back to the minivan. The groceries and two oldest children were already in the van, and she was just buckling Sammy into his car seat, when a man's voice behind her said, "Excuse me, ma'am."

Startled, she slammed the van door shut as she whirled to face him. Her first impression put her at immediate ease. His appearance was the very opposite of threatening. He was just barely taller than she (and she stood only 5' 3") and he was a bit on the fluffy side. He looked to be about forty, yet he still had chubby baby cheeks. His short, curly brown hair clung close to his head, and he wore relaxed-fitting jeans and a faded T-shirt. "Can I help you?" she asked.

"Sorry to bother you," he said with perfect pleasantness. "I just need to ask you a question, and I know it's going to sound strange, but it's very important." He paused.

"Okay?" she prodded.

"I need to know what the referee said to you before he died."

"He died?" She hadn't known that. They'd whisked him away into an ambulance so fast, she'd thought he'd had a good chance.

"I'm afraid that he did."

A thought occurred to her, and she scowled at the pleasant parking lot interloper. "Did the ref send you?"

He scowled back. "The ref has gone to heaven, ma'am."

She couldn't help it. She laughed so suddenly that she snorted. *What a strange way to remind me that he'd died.* "I meant the other ref."

"Oh!" her new friend said. "No, no, he didn't send me."

"Well, the poor old man didn't say anything to me," she said, again not knowing why she was lying, and opened her car door.

Her new friend reached over her and shut the door. If anyone else had done this, it might have been scary, but she didn't think this man could possibly scare her. Still, she found him quite rude. "Excuse me!" she said, but at the same exact time, he said, "You're lying," so she said, "Excuse me?!" again to defend herself against such an absolutely accurate accusation.

"You're lying," he repeated. "And that's really okay. I understand why you're lying"—

You do? Because I don't.

—"but I really need you to tell me the truth. It's important. And you can trust me."

In an instant, an overwhelming, supernatural peace flooded over her. Somehow she knew this was true. She could trust him. But she still didn't want to tell him her secret. "Who are you?"

"My name is Bob."

"Well, Bob, I don't know you. And it is raining. And I am not wearing a raincoat. And I need to get home before my ice cream melts." She started to open the door again. Again, he put his hand on it and prevented her from doing so. This time, she tried to pull it open anyway, against his resistance, but the door didn't budge. *This small man is stronger than he looks.* She looked him in the eye. His eyes were brown, soft, and gentle. "Get your hand off my car or I will tell my son to call the police."

He didn't move his hand. He looked in the car and said, "Your ten-year-old has a cell phone?"

"How do you know my son is ten, and no, he is currently playing a game on *my* cell phone.

13

Last warning. I will tell him to call—" She stopped talking because she saw a police officer crossing the parking lot. She started to call out "Officer!" but Bob clamped a hand over her mouth so all she got out was "Off!" which was also appropriate in this case. She pushed him in the chest. "Do not touch me!" Then she tried to hail the cop again.

Again he placed his hand over her mouth, but this time he held it there and leaned in close to whisper to her. "Don't do that! You're just going to make a fool of yourself, and I don't want to cause you any trouble."

He sounded sincere enough, but she couldn't believe he could mean such words while he was actively trying to smother her. She brought her knee up fast, homing in on his groin area, but he seemed to know it was coming and twisted his hips to protect himself. She longingly watched the police officer getting farther and farther away.

She saw a woman approaching a pickup parked nearby. Sandra widened her eyes at the woman as if to plead for help but the woman just looked at her as if she was looking at a crazy person and hurriedly got into her truck.

"I will explain," Bob said, "but you've got to promise not to draw any more attention to us."

Sandra nodded quickly.

Bob removed his hand.

"They can't see me," he said. "Only you can see me."

For several seconds, Sandra did not respond to this. Then she said, slowly, "I beg your pardon?"

"No one else can see me. Only you. Even your kids can't see me. Actually, the baby can, but Peter and Joanna can't. If they weren't staring at screens right now, they'd wonder why their mother was standing in the parking lot talking to herself while their ice cream melts."

Sandra looked through the window at Sammy, who was chewing on his fingers and grinning foolishly. Then she looked at Bob. "Why can Sammy see you?"

"All babies can see me." He took a deep breath. "Sandra, I'm an angel of the Lord, and I really need you to tell me what Frank Fenton said to you before he died."

Sandra burst into laughter. She tipped her head back and laughed at the sky. Raindrops splatted onto her closed eyelids. She hooted until she had to gasp for air.

"Are you finished?" Bob interrupted.

She looked at him through teary eyes. "An angel?"

He frowned. "Yes. An angel. Watch." He held out his hand and his palm burst into flames. Then just as quickly, it went out. Bob looked bored.

"Neat trick," Sandra said dryly.

"Sandra, I know you are a believer. Can we not drag this part out?"

Suddenly, Sandra knew. A weird certainty flowed through her, and she just knew beyond a shadow of a doubt that this man before her was a heavenly being. This knowledge brought on another bout of laughter. "I'm sorry," she managed between cackles, "I believe you, I do, I'm just … I'm just a little …" She tried to stop laughing. She had pictured angels before. This wasn't it.

"It can be overwhelming to meet an angel face to face, I know. Now, please tell me what he said."

"Why?" Sandra asked, trying to catch her breath.

"Why what?" She hadn't known angels could look so annoyed.

"Why do you need to know?"

"Because I'm an angel, that's why."

"But doesn't God know? Can't he just tell you?"

Bob looked embarrassed.

"What?" she prodded.

"I'd like to handle this on my own, if possible."

"I always get into trouble when I try to handle things on my own, without God. Are you in trouble, Bob?"

He flushed red. "I am not. But I have a job to do, and I would like to do it."

"What job?"

"Will you puh-lease just tell me what he said?"

"Sure, as soon as you tell me what your job is." She was rapidly growing more comfortable with this alleged angel.

Bob appeared to be weighing his options. Then he said, "It was my job to protect the souls involved in that soccer game."

She gasped. "So you *are* in trouble!"

"I don't know. That's why I need to know what he said."

She decided to stop torturing him. "He said, 'You've got to stop white.'"

"That's it?"

"That's it."

And Bob was gone. There was no bright light, no puff of smoke—he just vanished. He just wasn't there anymore. Sandra looked around the parking lot, suddenly self-conscious of how she must have appeared to everyone for the past several minutes. But no one seemed to be paying her any mind. She shakily climbed into the van, thinking her kids would chide her for taking so long, but they just continued to stare at their screens. "Peter?"

"Yeah?" He didn't look up.

"Can you please put the phone away?"

Peter sighed dramatically and turned the screen off.

"Thank you. Now, can you please tell me what has happened in your immediate vicinity since we came out of the store?"

"Uh, we came out of the store, we got in the car, and then you told me to turn the phone off."

"That's it?"

"That's it."

"Peter, you are grounded from all electronics."

"What?" he shrieked. "Why?"

"Because your mother could have been murdered by a random lunatic, and you wouldn't even have noticed. You would have just sat here until the phone battery died."

Peter was quiet for a minute. Sandra could feel him fuming behind her. Finally, he said, "How long?"

"How long before the battery would have died? How should I know?"

"No, how long am I grounded?"

"Oh. That. Forever."

Chapter 3

Sandra couldn't wait to tell her husband about her supernatural parking lot encounter, but when the time came, she was scared to bring it up. She wasn't sure if he would believe her. To her knowledge, he'd never doubted anything she'd told him before, but this? This would require a whole new level of faith in his wife.

So, when they finally crawled into bed late that evening, Nate said, "You've been awfully quiet. Everything okay?"

She sat up and scooted back to lean against the headboard. "Actually, I wanted to tell you something, but I'm kind of scared to."

He laughed. "Scared? You shouldn't be scared. You can tell me anything. You know that."

She took a deep breath and then let it all spill out: "So what Peter didn't tell you is that the referee ended up dying, and he said something to me before he did, but it wasn't any big deal. But people saw him say something, and they thought it was a big deal. The other ref asked me what he said. And then I was approached in the grocery store parking lot by a man named Bob, only he wasn't a man ..." She took another big breath. "And this is the part I'm scared to tell you. He was an angel, Nate, an honest-to-God angel. As soon as he told me, I just knew it was true—"

She stopped. She didn't like the look on Nate's face. Amused. Condescending. Entertained.

"Fine." She lay back down and rolled away from him. "I told you that you wouldn't believe me."

He gently shook her shoulder. "Hey, don't do that. I do believe you."

She looked over her shoulder at him. "No, you don't."

"Well, I'm not sure he was really an angel, but I believe that you thought he was."

"Never mind. I'm sorry that I told you."

"Hey, Sandra, don't do that. Don't pick a fight. I do believe you, but come on, the guy wasn't really an angel. Angels don't hang out at the Piggly Wiggly."

They didn't even have Piggly Wiggly stores in Maine, but Nate thought the name was hilarious and called all grocery stores Piggly Wiggly. When they'd first started dating, she'd found that adorable.

She squeezed her eyes shut, wishing she could rewind time about twenty minutes.

"Would you please finish your story?"

"That was it. That's the end of the story."

"An angel approached you and then didn't say anything?"

"He asked me what the ref had said, and I told him."

"And what did the ref say?"

"He said we had to stop the white team."

"Why would he say that?" He sounded critical, as if she was making up a story that didn't make sense.

"I don't know," Sandra said in a tone bordering on cranky. "I think he was delirious. The game was really physical, lots of elbows. Maybe he thought white was being too rough. The man was dying. His brain might not have been in tip-top shape."

"Did he have a heart attack?"

"I don't know. He was a hundred and five years old. I don't want to talk about it anymore. I'm tired." She closed her eyes again.

He took the hint, lay down himself, and turned off the light. "Good night," he said. She didn't answer. A few minutes later, he said,

"We've got to get up early tomorrow. It's my turn to teach Sunday school."

She groaned. Not because she didn't want to get up early, although she didn't. Not because she didn't enjoy Sunday school, because she did, but because she was frequently annoyed with how involved Nate was with everything and everyone other than his own family. He didn't neglect them or anything; he showed up to the major events. But he seemed to find the day-to-day grind beneath him. But if the church, or his school, or the multiple nonprofits he volunteered for needed him, he was Mr. Service. She squeezed her eyes shut tighter, trying to rein in her thoughts. She didn't want to mentally complain about her husband. She loved him. He was a good man, a good husband, a good father. And while mentally cataloging all his attributes, she drifted off to sleep.

Chapter 4

"I'm sick," Peter said.

"I'm sorry to hear that," Sandra replied, distracted. "I'll call your coach and let him know you won't be at practice this afternoon."

"No!" Peter said quickly, and then realized he was betraying himself and said more slowly, "I might be better by then. Don't call him yet."

She looked at her son. "You're going to church." The look on his face concerned her. He looked more crestfallen than he should have looked from such a benign pronouncement. "Honey, why don't you want to go to church?"

He shrugged and looked at the floor.

She gently lifted his chin toward her. His eyes came with it. "Sweetie, you know why we go to church, right?"

"Because there's power in group worship, and because iron sharpens iron," he recited dutifully, sounding too much like a robot.

She smiled, proud of his response even if it hadn't come from the heart. "That's right. So we need to go, okay?"

"Okay. Can I sit with you instead of going to junior church?"

This surprised her. "Of course you can. Why?"

"Junior church is for babies," he said and walked away, presumably to get ready for church.

Sandra went to refill her coffee mug, and Nate started hollering at everybody to hurry up. She looked at the clock. "We've still got plenty of time."

"I can't be late. I'm teaching today."

She closed her eyes to avoid rolling them. "I know that. But we're not going to be late. We've still got fifteen minutes before we have to leave."

"I want to leave now, Sandra, so we're not running in right at the bell"—

She hated it when he used school metaphors.

—"and so that I can be friendly and greet people when they walk in."

Thinking that he could stand to be a little more "friendly" with his own family, she resignedly dumped her coffee into a travel mug and went to get the baby.

Seven minutes later, Nate, in even more of a tizzy, climbed into the minivan's driver's seat and asked Sandra to hurry up with buckling Sammy in.

"Sorry, this thing has seventy-five snaps."

"You use hyperbole too much," he said, looking at his phone.

She had heard this complaint before, didn't remember what hyperbole meant, kept forgetting to look it up, and so never tempered her use of it.

"Shoot!" Peter cried and reached to open the sliding door. "I forgot my iPad."

From the front, Nate pressed a button that shut the door Peter had just started to open. "You don't need to bring your iPad to church."

"Dad, it's got my Bible on it!"

Nate leaned back against the headrest and hit the button again to open the door. "Fine. Hurry up."

Peter jumped out of the car and ran back inside. Sandra climbed into the front. "It's okay. We've got plenty of time."

"Doesn't that kid own a print Bible?"

"Of course he does. He has like six of them. But all the kids are using tablets for their Bibles at church."

"That's just foolish. We don't even let them have tablets in school."

"I know, but this isn't school."

Peter reappeared and climbed back into the van. Nate started to back out of the garage before the sliding door had even clicked shut.

"Thank you for hurrying, honey," Sandra said over her shoulder. Peter ignored her gratitude. He just stared out his window like he was on the way to the coal mines.

Church was only a few miles away. They pulled into the parking lot, which wasn't crowded yet, as many people didn't go to Sunday school, and of those who did, the majority showed up late. Nate parked close to the door and then wordlessly jumped out and headed inside, leaving Sandra to unpack the children. Peter was helpful, though, and grabbed the diaper bag without being asked. Then he followed her to the nursery, while Joanna ran off to find her class. There was no one in the nursery yet. *Of course there isn't. Because we're early.* Sandra sat in a rocking chair. "You can head to class, Peter. I'll wait for the nursery person to get here."

"I'll wait!" Peter chirped.

Sandra looked up, shocked. "What?"

"Dad's teaching today. I know he wouldn't want you to be late. So I'll wait with Sammy if you want."

Sandra looked at Sammy's chubby, drooly face and then at Peter's. "Are you sure?"

"Yeah. Definitely." He held out both hands for his little brother.

"Wow, Peter. Thanks. You are a good big brother." She handed the baby to him and got up. Peter immediately took her seat. Sandra left her two sons in the otherwise empty nursery, beaming with pride.

No one had shown up yet for Nate's adult Sunday school class, but they did start drifting in soon after Sandra joined him. She greeted her friends warmly, genuinely excited to see them.

Nate did a great job teaching the class. He was organized, a good communicator, and had a good sense of humor. Sandra admired him while he taught. She was proud of him. He'd taught high school math for ten years before becoming a principal. At first, he'd had no aspirations of going into administration, but then he thought it could be his gift to the world. There was so much need in the public schools, and he had such a servant's heart. He was a good principal—a great one even. He'd made a lot of positive changes in their school district's high school, and was respected by all the teachers and most of the students and parents. Sandra hadn't weighed in on the decision, had thought he probably knew best about whether to make the move from teacher to administrator, but she now believed he'd made the right decision.

When class finished, Sandra went back to the nursery to check on Sammy, and found Peter still there, holding his brother. "Peter! What are you still doing here?" The nursery was now full of tiny humans, not Peter's favorite demographic, and Odetta, this week's nursery volunteer, was also there, directing toddler traffic.

"Oh, Sandra! Thank God for this little saint of yours!" she gushed, tousling Peter's hair with her free hand.

Peter blushed, and Sandra couldn't believe he didn't flinch away from her slightly invasive display of affection.

"He has stayed with me the whole time, and he's been such a huge help! Can he help more often? He's been rockin' babies and wipin' hineys!"

Sandra's jaw dropped. Peter had never changed a diaper in his life. What on earth was going on?

Chapter 5

Thanks to Sammy, Sandra was up early on Monday morning, and though she was exhausted, it was nice to enjoy the soft early morning sunshine streaming through her kitchen window—before the alarms went off and anarchy ensued. She had to get two kids dropped off at school on time while fighting the traffic of the hundreds of other mothers trying to do the same thing. She could put them on the school bus, of course, but she'd tried that years ago with Peter, and he'd learned far too much about the birds and the bees on that five-mile ride to school.

She took a gulp of her coffee and tried to focus on the psalm in front of her, but Mr. T kept sliding his body between her eyeballs and her Bible. Nate had named the cat Mr. T because of the thick black stripe down its back. When Sandra had reminded her husband that the cat was a female, Nate had said it was too late. The cat's name was Mr. T.

She placed the persistent animal on the floor for the fourth time and brought her Bible closer to her eyes. She tried to read, but after only a few lines, she was thinking about that poor referee again. What had Bob the angel said his name was? Frank Fenton. He'd been old, had probably died doing what he loved, and Bob had said he was in heaven. So, why did she feel so sad?

A tapping on the window startled her, but when she turned to look through said window, what she saw startled her even more. Did angels really need to knock? Maybe he *wasn't* an angel after all. No, he was. She knew it. She gave him a look that she hoped communicated both confusion and irritation. Her kids knew that look well. Bob didn't appear to understand. He pointed toward the door.

Shaking her head, she went to the door and cracked it open. "Why are you knocking on my window? You scared me."

"Sorry," he whispered. "I didn't want to wake everybody up."

She frowned, not understanding.

"If I knocked on the door," he explained, "it would be too loud. So, I saw you sitting there, and thought I would just need to tap on the glass to get your attention. And it worked." He looked smug. "Anyway, I need your help. Can we chat?"

She looked around her neighborhood. "I don't know, do people think I'm talking to myself right now?"

"If anyone's looking, then, yes. I should come inside."

She stepped out of his way and watched him softly close the door behind him. Part of her was elated at the idea of an angel in her home. Part of her wished he'd waited until she'd gotten dressed. She folded her arms across her chest self-consciously. "What can I do for you?"

"I need your help."

"You mentioned that."

"I'm in a bit of trouble, I think."

"Why? Trouble with whom?"

He stared upward. At first she thought he meant her family asleep upstairs. Then she understood. "Oh. God?" She glanced nervously at her ceiling. "Really?"

He nodded. "I shouldn't have left the soccer game, but I was overseeing several events at once, and there was a scuffle on the golf course."

She raised an eyebrow. "Golfers scuffle?" She found that difficult to believe.

He nodded adamantly. "But this wasn't a bad one. I should've stayed put. I should've known trouble was brewing."

"How could you have known the ref's heart was going to give out? Are angels psychic?"

"Frank Fenton didn't just drop dead of natural causes," he said, deftly dodging her second question.

"Are you saying there was foul play?" On some level, she knew she'd just made a pun, but she also knew it would be in incredibly poor taste to celebrate it.

"Poisoned."

Sandra gasped. "How do you know all this?"

"I hear things."

She considered that. "You mean, you can invisibly lurk in places and eavesdrop?"

He shrugged. "We're only supposed to do it when necessary, but yes."

"So, why can't you just lurk and eavesdrop and find out *who* poisoned him?"

Bob exhaled quickly. "We just can't, okay! There are rules that we have to follow, and we can't get to all places at all times to all people—"

"*We?* Just how many of you are there, Bob?"

"How many middle school sports angels?"

"No." *He's a bit daft for an angel of the Lord, isn't he?* "How many angels in all?"

His eyes widened just a little. "Many."

Wow, that was helpful. "I'm sorry to hear that he was killed on purpose, but I don't see how I can help." She was having trouble even believing the news. Who murders an ancient soccer ref?

He took a step closer to her, glancing at the stairs to make sure they weren't about to be interrupted by little feet. "I can't figure out what he meant. That you had to stop white? What did that mean?" He was so over the top with his earnestness that she almost laughed at him, but a man had been killed.

"It meant," she said slowly, "that he wanted someone to stop the white team. They were fouling a lot."

Bob scowled. "It doesn't make any sense."

Sandra didn't say anything. What did this guy want from her? *Angel*, she corrected herself. What did this *angel* want from her? "I know it doesn't make any sense, but he was dying. He probably wasn't in his right mind. Or maybe he was really dedicated to the job."

"I need you to talk to his wife."

Sandra laughed in his face. "Absolutely not."

"Come on, I really shouldn't do it."

"I'm assuming that the conversation you overheard involved law enforcement? So, the police know that he was murdered? So, let them figure it out. That's their job."

Bob shook his head dramatically. "It's my fault he died. I need to—"

"It's not your fault!" Sandra cried, too loudly. "How could you possibly stop a poisoning?"

"I don't know," Bob said, also too loudly. "All I know is that he died on my watch, and I need to show some initiative and try to set things right."

Sandra didn't know what to say. She was most certainly not going to talk to some grieving widow. "Just out of curiosity, how old is his wife?" she asked, thinking she too had to be ancient and might really be in need with her husband gone. Maybe she *should* go see her, just to check on her.

"Twenty-six." He cocked his head to the side and raised his eyebrows.

Sandra almost tipped over backward and grabbed the stair banister for support. "You're kidding. He had to have been at least eighty."

"Seventy-nine to be precise. I'm telling you. Something hinky is going on. Please, help me."

She raised an eyebrow. "Is this God asking me or is it you?"

"Not God," Bob said quickly.

"Is God going to be upset with me for helping you?"

"Absolutely not." He sounded so sure.

But could *she* be sure? Why was she even considering this? This was madness. But she had to admit, she was curious. And as busy as her life was, she was also often bored. This intrigued her. Plus, she liked hanging out with an angel. "I'll have to think about it."

"No time for that."

"Mom?" A squeaky voice called down the stairs. "Who are you talking to?"

"I'll be back," Bob whispered, and then he was gone.

Chapter 6

When Sandra returned from dropping the kids off at school, struggling under the weight of the baby carrier hanging off her hand, she looked up to see Bob sitting on her porch swing. She knew she should be annoyed by his persistence, but she was happy to see him. How many people can say they've been stalked by an angel? "I suppose you're invisible to everyone but me?"

He nodded and smiled. "Everyone but you and Sammy."

Sandra looked down at her son, who was smiling broadly and gazing right at Bob.

"Are you ready to go?" Bob asked.

Sandra took a deep breath. Part of her wanted to do this. Part of her knew it was sheer madness. "I'm not sure I'm the right girl for the job."

"I'll be right there beside you."

She came up the steps, set Sammy down so he could still see Bob's face, and joined the angel on the swing. She stretched her legs out in front of her and looked at Bob, who was making silly faces at Sammy. "What exactly are you expecting us to find out at the widow's house?"

Bob shrugged. "I have no idea. Maybe she killed him."

What? This angel was nuts. "You want me to have a chat with a murderer?"

"Like I said, I'll be right there with you."

That didn't make Sandra feel much better. "What do you want me to ask her? Hey, I'm sorry for your loss, but did you kill your husband?"

"No, I can't help but think there was more meaning to his final words than you think. Maybe she'll know something about it. Just go and offer your condolences, tell her you're really upset about it, and tell her that you thought she might want to hear his final words." This all came out quickly. He had obviously thought this through.

Was she really considering this? She looked down at Sammy. "I'm not taking my baby to visit a murderer's house."

"Of course not. Is there a grandparent you could leave him with?"

That was annoying. "Sure. In Ohio."

He frowned and looked around the neighborhood, apparently scanning for anyone who looked like they wanted to babysit an infant right now.

"Never mind. I know a homeschooled teen from church. Let me give her a call."

An hour later, Sandra was driving down the road with an invisible passenger. Was she losing her mind? This was too unreal.

"Don't feel guilty about leaving Sammy. He'll be fine."

Sandra's eyes snapped toward Bob. "Can you read my mind?"

He put one hand on the dashboard. "Look at the road, please."

She snickered. "Why? Are you afraid of crashing? Can't you just disappear at the last second?"

"I'm not afraid of me crashing. I'm afraid of you crashing.

"Okay, I appreciate the concern, but you didn't answer my question. Can you read my mind?" She really didn't like that idea.

"Of course not. I can see your face. You have the guilty mom look, but you have nothing to feel guilty about. You never leave your baby, and you're only doing it this time because you're doing a really big favor for an angel."

A thought occurred to her. "Why don't you just do it? Why do you need me? Why don't you just appear to her and ask her questions?"

"Because you have an in. You were there when he died." He paused. "Besides," he said, his voice growing so quiet she could barely hear him, "we're really not supposed to appear to people unless it's absolutely necessary."

"It was absolutely necessary for you to appear to me in the Piggly Wiggly parking lot and make my ice cream melt?" Oh great. Now she was doing the stupid Piggly Wiggly thing too.

He squirmed in his seat. "Like I said, I might be in a bit of trouble here. This hasn't been my finest hour."

She felt bad for him then and stopped interrogating him. She pulled her minivan into the driveway of a very nice home. It wasn't a mansion, but it was big and modern and looked expensive. "What did he do for work, other than refereeing?"

Bob vanished, and for a second Sandra panicked that he had left her. Then she realized that he'd just gotten out of the car. Of course. Why would an angel open the door? She got out of her car the non-supernatural way, and Bob answered her, "He's retired."

"I could've guessed that much. What did he do before he was retired?"

"He was a teacher."

She looked up at the house and then back to Bob. "You're kidding. Well, his wife must make a lot of money."

"I don't think she works." Bob cast her a knowing glance. "Like I said, something hinky. Also, you should stop talking to me, in case she's looking out a window."

Sandra took a deep breath. Having an imaginary friend was going to take some getting used to. Maybe she should ask Joanna for some pointers.

Chapter 7

Sandra lifted a trembling hand to knock on the late referee's door. What was she doing? She didn't do stuff like this! It was entirely irrational. It occurred to her then that maybe Bob was using some supernatural mind control over her. She looked at him over her shoulder and opened her mouth to ask, but he shook his head slightly. Oh yeah, she probably shouldn't talk to him right now. She returned her attention to the door, which was still shut. How long was she supposed to stand here and wait? She'd never felt more foolish, and yet, there was a weird thrill coursing through her veins too. As absurd as this was, she was having a bit of fun.

She was about to give up and leave when a sports car pulled into the driveway and a long-legged blonde climbed out. "Can I help you?" she asked, sounding notably suspicious.

Sandra froze. What was she supposed to say again? Why was she here again?

The woman approached, scowling, her arms laden with shopping bags from multiple department stores. She came up the steps with a confidence Sandra envied. "Who are you?"

Suddenly, Bob was standing very close behind her. Had he crept up on her or just materialized there? She didn't know, but the hand he placed on her shoulder brought incredible reassurance. "I'm sorry, I'm not very good at this sort of thing," she stammered.

"What sort of thing might that be?"

This woman was unpleasant. *She's grieving*, Sandra reminded herself. *I think.* "I was there … when your husband died, and I'm so sorry for your loss, but I just … I'm really shaken by the whole thing, and well …" She glanced at the closed door. "Could we talk inside?"

The woman hesitated.

"Only for a minute."

With body language that made it clear she wasn't into the whole thing, she unlocked the door and swung it open so that Sandra could step inside first. Suddenly, Sandra was sure the widow was going to stab her in the back. If that happened, would Bob protect her? *Could* Bob protect her? He didn't look like much of a fighter. Did he have an invisible sword tucked away somewhere?

Sandra stepped into the cool darkness and then stepped aside until the woman could join her. "My name is Sandra. Your husband was reffing my son's soccer game when he died."

The woman dropped her keys on a counter and set her packages down on a bench. "Isabelle," she said, without looking at Sandra. "And?"

"And ..." Really, what *was* the and? Why was she here again? "And, well, I was the last person he spoke to before he died"—

Isabelle's eyes snapped to attention at that.

—"and that's kind of a personal moment, and I thought you'd like to know what he said."

"I would like to know," she said with notable eagerness.

Sandra took a shaky breath. Oh boy, no turning back now. "He said, 'You've got to stop white.'"

Barely a flicker, but it was there. That meant something to this woman. But what? What could that possibly mean other than the interpretation Sandra had? "Is that all?" Isabelle asked.

Sandra nodded. "I'm sorry. I wish there were more. It just seemed like such a strange thing to say, and I thought, as his wife, you might want to know. If it were me, I would want to know my husband's last words."

Isabelle nodded. "Right, well, thanks for stopping by." She put one hand to Sandra's back as if to shoo her out of the foyer. Was that fear in her voice?

Sandra stood firm. "Does that mean anything to you?"

"No, nothing at all," she said quickly. Too quickly.

Sandra tried not to look suspicious. She didn't want to tip her hand.

"He'd been saying lots of weird things lately. Getting older, you know," she said, as if she had the first idea about what it meant to get older.

"I see." Sandra looked at Bob for further cues, but he was just standing there.

"So, is that all?" Isabelle opened the door.

"Uh … yes. Thank you. Again, I just wanted to say sorry for your loss. If there's anything I can do, just—"

"Thank you." She slammed the door in Sandra's face.

She stood there for a second and then turned toward the driveway. Bob had already seated himself in her passenger seat. He was an assuming angel, wasn't he?

She had the sudden urge to leap over the steps and run to her minivan, but she forced herself to take normal, even steps. Once she'd backed out into the road, though, she turned to Bob. "Did you see that? She flinched when I said the thing about the white team! She totally knew something! She was hiding something!" She slammed the steering wheel with her open palm. "I knew it!" Then she wondered why she'd just said that. She hadn't known anything at all.

"If I didn't know better, I'd think you were enjoying this."

Sandra tried to keep the joy out of her voice. "Would you prefer I be miserable?"

He shook his head. "Of course not. I just think it's funny that you're having fun. Anyway, you're right. She did flinch. She does know something. But whereas she won't tell us what she knows, I don't see how that little visit helped us much." He made it sound as though the whole thing had been her idea, and had been a bad one. This was obnoxious.

Even worse, she felt defensive of the idea. "It helped us by suggesting that she's the one who killed him."

"Then I'm off the hook," he said matter-of-factly.

"What?" What hook was he off, exactly?

"If she's the one who killed him, she didn't do it on the soccer field, so it's not my fault—"

"Is that all you care about?" she cried, indignant. Then she folded her lips in. She'd just interrupted an angel. Maybe that wasn't advisable.

"Of course not. But if it's not my fault, then I'll let the police do their thing. I don't need to try to make up for my lack of diligence if it wasn't my lack of diligence that got him killed."

This made perfect sense, of course. But it also made part of Sandra sad. She didn't want to leave it up to the police. She wanted to figure out the puzzle herself. "We need more information," she said, mostly to herself.

"We do. And I have no idea where to get it."

"Me neither." They rode along in silence for several minutes. Then she remembered the mind control. She cleared her throat. How should she phrase her question, exactly?

"Go ahead, spit it out."

"I thought you couldn't read my mind."

"I can't, but I'm intuitive enough to know you have something on your mind."

"I was just wondering … do angels … I mean … *can* angels do … mind control?"

He barked out a laugh. "Of course not!"

She breathed a sigh of relief. "Excellent."

He was still laughing. This annoyed her. It hadn't been *that* stupid of a question. She decided to ask him another question, to get his mind off her last one. "Peter has another home game today. Is that one of yours?"

"It sure is. Middle school soccer has never made me so nervous."

She cocked an eyebrow at him. "Are you serious? Haven't you been battling big scary demons for millennia?"

He shook his head. "Nope. Those weren't my missions."

"Really. So what kind of missions did you do in Old Testament times? They didn't have middle school soccer then, right?"

But Bob didn't answer, and when she looked in his direction, he was gone.

That trick was going to get annoying.

Chapter 8

Missing the adrenaline rush she'd just experienced, Sandra stepped into her home to find Sammy screaming in the Pack 'n Play and the teenager watching *Pretty Little Liars* on Netflix. Gritting her teeth, she forced a smile at the young woman, handed her a small amount of cash that was still too much, and bid her adieu. Then she scooped Sammy up to find his diaper soaked. Guilt rushed over her. What had she been doing, acting like some kind of secret super sleuth? She was a mom. She didn't have time for other adventures—motherhood was enough of an adventure in and of itself.

She got the new diaper in place and then squeezed her son to her chest. "I'm sorry, punkin. I shouldn't have left you." She kissed him on his soft temple and soaked in the miraculous smell of him. This was enough. For a moment, she'd thought her life was too boring, but this was enough. She moved Sammy to her left hip, and he flashed her a giant gummy smile. "Want to go help me make the pot roast?" She would be far too tired to cook when she got home that night, so she wanted to get supper going now. Thank the Lord for Crock-Pots.

She pushed his walker into the kitchen with her toe and then began the slow, complex task of putting Sammy's chubby legs through the small holes. She'd get one in, and he'd curl the other one up and into himself like a shy, stubborn turtle leg. Then, as she unfolded that leg and stuck it in the hole, the first would *boing* back up to his waist. This was a game they played, and, though Sandra had long grown tired of it, she knew too that this season would soon pass and she'd be dealing with Sammy's stinky soccer cleats instead. With Sammy finally nestled into his colorful fabric seat, she turned toward the cutting board.

As she chopped garlic, onions, carrots, and potatoes, Sammy babbled nonsensically beside her, and she thought about poor Mr. Frank Fenton and his mysteriously young wife. Sandra silently scolded herself. An age discrepancy didn't necessarily mean that something sordid was going on. Maybe Isabelle liked older men, or maybe Frank Fenton was just that good of a catch, no matter what his age. Or maybe there was simply no accounting for taste.

Her phone rang, startling her out of her thoughts so suddenly that her knife slipped and she almost parted with her thumb. She looked at Sammy. "Now, where did I put my phone?"

He stared at her with wide eyes. If he knew the cell's location, he wasn't giving it up. She knew it was close; she could hear it loud and clear—but where *was* the blasted thing? It sounded as though it was coming from behind her. If she didn't find it soon, it would stop ringing. That wouldn't necessarily be a bad thing. She spun away from the counter to look, but then the ring sounded as though it was coming from the counter. What on earth?

It was then she realized that her butt was vibrating. Feeling foolish, she whipped the phone out of her back pocket and answered it in the nick of time, without looking at the caller ID. And so, she was doubly surprised when the school secretary identified herself. Her heart jumped into her throat. What was wrong? Peter was never sick, and if he was, he would call her himself. Visions of all the school crises that had ever happened flashed through her mind in a second.

"Everyone's fine," the secretary explained, "but there's been an incident, and Mrs. Van DeVenter would like to speak with you. Can you come in?"

"Of course," Sandra said before she really thought about it. What incident couldn't be discussed over the phone? Keeping her annoyance and resentment to herself, she promised to be there as soon as possible and then began the great project of getting the baby into his little autumn coat and his car seat.

By the time they were headed down the road toward the school, her resentment had blossomed into anger. What couldn't wait until the end of the day, when she would have gone to school to pick him up? And why hadn't she mentioned that when the secretary had called? Why hadn't she stuck up for herself, for her time?

She pulled into the crowded school parking lot, parked near the back, and then schlepped herself, her overburdened purse, her equally overburdened diaper bag, and the giant car seat to the front door of the elementary school, where she had to wait several minutes to be buzzed in. This too irritated her. They'd known she was coming. They'd invited her. And now they weren't letting her in.

As she was considering returning to her car and making a run for it, the door buzzed open. With a great effort to be pleasant, she checked in at the main office and was shown to a hard wooden bench outside the principal's closed door. This just kept getting better.

Sandra didn't yet know Mrs. Van DeVenter. This was her first year as principal of Mark Emery School, and Sandra tried to be patient, imagining how busy grades kindergarten through eighth could keep a person. She knew how busy grades nine through twelve kept her husband.

Sammy started to scream. She scooped him out of his car seat, but made no effort to shush him. People tended to work faster at customer service when Sammy screamed.

True to the pattern, Mrs. Van DeVenter opened the door and welcomed Sandra into her inner sanctum, where she found her eldest son with tear streaks down his face. Adrenaline gushed through her, and she surged into mama bear mode, rushing across the room to him. "What's wrong, honey? What happened?"

Peter's face sank toward the floor, and he flinched away from her touch.

Mrs. Van DeVenter shut the door, annoying Sandra again. The car seat and diaper bag were still on the bench. "Please, Mrs. Provost, have a seat. Thanks so much for coming in."

"Call me Sandra." She slid a chair over to Peter, as much to comfort him as to signal to the principal that she was firmly, unequivocally on her son's side. Peter was in trouble. She could see it on his face and feel it in the air. And though she knew her son was far from perfect, she also knew he didn't do things that landed him in the principal's office in tears.

"What happened?" Sandra asked the administrator, and Sammy echoed her question with a bellow that sounded highly critical.

Mrs. Van DeVenter rolled her chair close to her desk and then folded her hands on top of her blotter, which was covered with sticky notes. She took a long breath. "There's been an incident."

Yeah, I got that much.

"A bullying incident."

"No, there hasn't," Sandra said, proud of the quickness of her answer and the firmness in her voice. The principal's tone made it clear that Peter wasn't the victim, which meant she was accusing him of being the bully. That just wasn't possible. Sandra might not be good at sticking up for herself, but sticking up for her children? Piece of cake.

Chapter 9

"I beg your pardon?" Mrs. Van DeVenter said, sounding appropriately indignant.

Sandra leveled a gaze at the new principal. "I am far more concerned about my son's behavior than you are, and will be the first to correct him when he is wrong, but my son is no bully." This was the kid who liked helping out in the church nursery, for crying out loud.

She was obviously unimpressed. "I'm sorry, but Peter did, in fact, push a fourth grader to the ground. He's admitted it."

Sandra heard the words, but in no way accepted them. She turned to look at Peter, who looked scared to speak. Before she could coax him to do so, the principal started talking again.

"I'm afraid that we have a zero tolerance policy. Physical bullying is a two-day suspension."

Over my dead body. Sandra knew then that she would take this to the Supreme Court if necessary. "Peter," she said softly, trying to pretend the principal wasn't there and they weren't both sitting in the hot seats, "what happened?"

He shrugged, but he finally looked at her. "Cameron Thompson is a jerk."

Sandra recognized the name. Cameron had played with Peter in summer soccer. Cameron's mother was insufferable.

"*He's* the bully." Peter's voice wavered up and down.

Sandra's heart broke for him. This kid didn't know how to be in trouble and was obviously incredibly uncomfortable with it. She resisted the urge to throw her body between him and the mean principal. "Did you push him?" She tried to sound objective, rational. She almost made it.

Peter nodded. "He deserved it. I'd push him again."

Oh dear. That didn't sound like the Peter she was so stoutly defending. "What do you mean, honey?"

"I mean that he was threatening second graders, telling them he was going to make them eat poop if they didn't do what he told them to do, and he was telling them to do *bad* stuff. They would've gotten into trouble. I told

Cameron to leave them alone, but he wouldn't. So I pushed him away from them, and he fell down and acted like a drama queen, like I beat him up or something." Peter sniffed loudly.

Sandra turned her eyes to the principal. "Sounds to me like Peter wasn't the bully. Sounds like he was *defending* the *bullied*."

Mrs. Van DeVenter still looked unimpressed. "That may well be, but he still *pushed* the child."

Peter folded his arms across his chest and raised his chin. He simultaneously looked like her little baby and a young man.

Sandra's chest swelled with pride. "Even so, he was trying to do the right thing. Instead of humiliating him and forcing him to miss two days of his education, maybe we could use this opportunity to teach him how to better handle such a situation—"

"He should have gone to a teacher!" Mrs. Van DeVenter interrupted her.

"Why?" Peter cried. "Teachers never do anything about bullying! Adults don't ever do anything!" His voice went up several notes with each word until he was squeaking. "Adults don't care!" he cried.

Oh dear. This isn't helping. She'd never seen Peter so irreverent.

The principal gave her an I-told-you-so look that Sandra ignored.

She put a hand on her son's knee. "Honey, that's not true. *I care.* I *always* care. You can tell me about any of this, and I'll make sure bullying is addressed."

"We'd prefer he come to someone at school."

Sandra was suddenly *very* tired of her son's principal. "That would be great too, but I want him to know that if that doesn't work, he can come to me."

"I've told two different teachers," Peter mumbled, now back in control of his emotions. "This has been going on since the first day of school."

That wiped the smugness off the principal's face. The first day of school was a week ago. "Which teachers?"

Peter named them.

Sammy started screaming. Sandra recognized the cry. It was the I'm-tired-and-you're-not-letting-me-sleep complaint. "Under the circumstances," Sandra said, nearly hollering to be heard over Sammy's demands, "can we just give Peter a warning about getting physical, and let him get back to class now?"

Sammy got even louder. Sandra was so proud of both her sons. The three of them made a fairly persuasive team.

The principal appeared to be thinking it over. She looked at Peter. "Do you understand that what you did was wrong?" she asked, but her voice was barely audible.

Peter nodded, whether he heard her or not.

"You can't push people, no matter what they're doing. That's assault."

Sandra caught her eyes just in time, right before they were about to do a big roll. Assault? Come on, the kid was ten years old.

Peter nodded. "I won't do it again. I was just trying to stick up for the little kids."

Mrs. Van DeVenter nodded, looking contemplative. "All right. I appreciate that. But next time, don't get physical, and tell a teacher. I'll talk to the teachers and make sure they are taking bullying seriously. We're not going to suspend you—*this* time. But you are on probation. Do you know what that means?"

Peter nodded, even though Sandra knew he had no idea what that meant.

"You may, however, be suspended from today's soccer game. That will be up to your coach."

Chapter 10

Sandra was halfway home when Sammy fell asleep, so she just kept driving around in circles, waiting for her kids to get out of school. What a crazy day it had been. Her son was growing up. She was proud of him for standing up for the oppressed, for the downtrodden. She wasn't so proud of him for pushing a kid to the ground, but she wasn't exactly upset with him for that either. It sounded like the kid had it coming, and if Cameron's mother was any indication of Cameron's attitude, then she could understand perfectly why Peter had thought a good shove was appropriate. But she fervently hoped that the coach wouldn't make him ride the bench today. That wouldn't be fair, and Peter would take it hard.

Finally, she pulled her van into the front of what would soon be a long line of cars waiting for that final bell. As soon as her car stopped moving, Sammy opened his eyes, his mouth, and his lungs. Sandra took a deep breath, said, "We're just going to sit here for a minute, punkin, and then we'll get back on the road," and then turned her Casting Crowns CD up louder. Sammy loved Casting Crowns, and usually didn't cry when the pianist—Sandra thought her name was Megan—sang. They really should let her sing more often. She skipped ahead a few songs to one where Megan took the vocals, and sure enough, Sammy stopped screaming.

The bell rang, and kids spilled out of the front doors. Joanna was near the front, and Sandra's heart swelled at the sight of her sweet daughter. It had only been a few hours, but she'd missed her. Joanna ran for the car, her thin coat flapping out behind her. Peter came along shortly after, moving with much less enthusiasm. Sandra couldn't blame him.

The side door slid open, and Joanna started chattering as she dove for the middle seat. Sandra didn't really hear her; she was looking at Peter, who, sans expression, got into the front seat and immediately turned the music down. Sammy started screaming. She reached over and put a hand on her son's leg. "I love you."

"Love you too," he said without looking at her.

She started the engine and pulled out into the stream of minivans and SUVs heading away from the school. "Honey," she said, trying to tread carefully, knowing Peter would clam up if he felt she was nosing into his feelings, "when you said adults don't care about bullying, I just want you to know that *I* care." She sneaked a look at him. "You know that, right?"

He moved his head up and down, but it wasn't a convincing nod.

What did *that* mean? She considered her words carefully. "You say you know that, but it seems like you don't know that."

He sighed, his eyes trying to bore two holes through the windshield. "Can we just drop it, Mom?"

Her neck got hot. "No, we can*not* drop it. How can you think I don't care about bullying? Have you even met me?"

He finally looked at her and then glanced toward the backseat. "Can we not talk about it *now*?"

She turned some knobs and put Casting Crowns into the rear speakers. Then she cranked the volume.

Peter rolled his eyes. "She can still hear us."

Sandra looked in the rearview mirror and asked, "Anyone want ice cream?" Joanna didn't blink. "She can't hear us. Talk."

He sighed again. "I know you care, Mom. You care about *everything*." He managed to make this sound like a bad thing. "But you're also so busy that sometimes you don't know the bullying is going on."

What? "How could I know, Peter, if you don't tell me? I don't follow you around at school all day." She'd thought about doing that several times since that first day she'd dropped him off five years ago, but she'd managed to restrain herself.

"I'm not talking about school," he said so quietly that she wondered if she'd heard him wrong.

She paused, knowing that if she asked him to repeat himself, he would be beyond annoyed. "Then what *are* you talking about?"

"Nothing. Just forget about it."

She pulled the van into the parking lot of a lingerie boutique. Peter's eyes widened in panic.

"What are we doing at a fancy underwear store?" Joanna piped up.

Sandra ignored her and turned to face her son. "I'm not going to forget about it. Just tell me what's going on and then this conversation can be over and you can stop feeling so uncomfortable."

"Yeah, right." His sarcasm was thicker than her sister-in-law's makeup.

She didn't flinch. She just kept staring at him. Sammy started screaming again. Sandra turned the music up.

"It's too loud!" Joanna cried.

She could see Peter's resolve weakening. She would never allow one of her children to be more stubborn than she was, and Peter knew it.

"Church, okay? I'm talking about church."

She recoiled. "What? Someone's being bullied at church?" That was the *last* place she'd worry about.

"Not someone," he muttered.

Oh no. A vision of him hiding in the nursery flashed through her mind. "Someone at church is picking on *you*—"

"Don't say 'picking on.' It makes me sound like I'm five."

"Okay, so what's going on?"

"People are jerks, and I'm not naming names, so don't try to make me."

"Peter James, you tell me right now. Unless you want to sit right here in this exact spot through your game and then through supper and then through the night—"

"Ethan and Jack," he spat out. "And more. Everyone follows them." He finally looked her in the eye. "It doesn't matter. There's nothing we can do about it. They won't stop. Now, can we please just go home?"

She gazed at him for nearly a minute, weighing her options. Her first choice was to drive to each of their houses, invite them outside, and then thump them on the head repeatedly, but she thought this might be ineffective and get her thrown in the clink. Peter was obviously done talking. She needed to talk to Nate. He'd know what to do. "Of course, honey, we can go home. Thank you for telling me. And we *will* do something about it. Church is supposed to be a safe place."

"Yeah, right," he said again.

Chapter 11

Ten minutes into the first half, Peter still hadn't been put in the game. This was weird; even though he was only a wee fifth grader, he was one of the best players, and he'd started in their last game. She had a bad feeling in her stomach. This had to be about the incident at school. She forced herself to wait until halftime to do anything, and then she waited for the team meeting to be over before approaching the coach.

She didn't want to approach the coach. She knew Peter would hate her for it. But he shouldn't be benched for defending little kids.

She asked a nearby mom to watch her two youngest, and the woman looked up from her phone just long enough to grudgingly agree. Joanna whined. She wanted to go with her, but Sandra didn't know how this was going to go, and didn't need a little distraction, nor a little audience, hanging off her hand.

Her stomach full of butterflies, she walked the seventeen-mile-long goal line and then rounded the corner to head for the bench. The coach saw her coming and pretended he didn't.

"Hi, Mr. Bell," she called out, "do you have a second?"

"A quick one. The game's about to start."

This was not true. There were five minutes on the clock. Did he think she couldn't read a clock?

"I just wanted to check in with you. There was an incident at school today, and I didn't know if you'd heard—"

"Of course I've heard. Mrs. Van DeVenter lets me know whenever my athletes get into trouble at school."

"Great," she lied. "Well, I just wanted to make sure you heard Peter's side of it—"

He held up a patronizing hand. "There is no *Peter's side*. He pushed a kid, and he will spend this game on the bench as a consequence. He's lucky I let him suit up." He would have had to work incredibly hard to sound more self-righteous.

She raised an eyebrow. "Lucky? Do you know that he was sticking up for some second-graders who were getting picked on? Do you know that he didn't mean to knock Cameron down, that he was just trying to protect the younger boys?" She knew her voice was getting louder and higher-pitched, but she couldn't seem to stop it. It was like a runaway train.

He held up the hand again, but she ignored it.

"Of *course* we should talk to him about better ways to prevent bullying, but I don't think benching him for an entire game is an appropriate—"

"*I* decide what is and isn't appropriate around here, ma'am. And I can't encourage my athletes to engage in vigilante justice on the playground."

"Vigilante?" she shrieked. This kept getting more and more absurd. A gentle voice in her head reminded her that she was representing Jesus to everyone watching this scene. What would Jesus do? When he got angry at injustice, he flipped over tables. Maybe she could flip over the bench. How heavy was that thing? The scorer's table looked more manageable.

"Everything okay here?" a man's voice interrupted.

Sandra turned to see one of the officials giving her an official-looking stare down.

She was going to lose this battle. She knew it then. The men were ganging up on her, and maybe they should. She was, after all, the crazy mom hollering at the coach. She was being the mom she'd sworn she'd never be. But darn it, she *needed* to be a little crazy right now. This situation was crazy.

The official stuck out his hand. "Michael White."

Her breath caught, and all fury fled her brain. "I'm sorry, what?"

His hand was still stuck out in the air, so she took it and allowed him to pump hers up and down. His hand was very wet, as were his shirt and forehead. "I said, my name is Michael White. And you are?"

"Sandra."

"Well, Sandra, the game is about to start, and no non-team personnel are allowed in this area. If you could find your way back to the spectator section, that'd be great."

She nodded, totally forgetting about Peter's situation. She backed away, still staring at the referee, who now had his back to her and was blowing his whistle. Finally, she turned and headed away, picking up her pace. She hadn't accomplished her mission. Peter was still benched. But she wasn't thinking about that. She wasn't even thinking about the fact that her son was being bullied at church. She could now think of only one thing: the soccer official's name. Michael *White.*

Chapter 12

Nate was frequently late to dinner, but Sandra was more annoyed with him tonight than she usually was. Her brain was bursting with things to talk to him about, and he was at yet another meeting.

"When's Daddy getting home?" Joanna asked with a pout. Was she feeling the same thing Sandra was or just mimicking Sandra's own unspoken sentiment?

Sandra didn't know. "He'll be here soon, honey. We can start eating without him." She usually made them wait, but the pot roast was already dry enough to serve as kindling. She should have made gravy. Sometime between interviewing grieving widows and fighting with principals and coaches.

Sandra scooped food onto four of the five plates, giving Sammy only some mushy carrots for now, and then sat next to the head of the table. The beef didn't look very appetizing, but that wasn't the end of the world. She wasn't hungry. Neither, apparently, was Peter, judging from the way he was pushing his food around on the plate. She could hardly blame him. He'd had a rough day. She started to cut up some small beef bites for Sammy.

"Is there any gravy?" Joanna whined.

"No," Sandra said with more sharpness than she'd meant to. Great. Add a splash of guilt to the whirlpool of emotions swirling around in her head. Her short fuse led to a long, sad silence that remained unbroken until they heard the sound of Nate's engine pulling into the driveway. Sandra's heart leapt at the sound of it. After all these years, she still got excited to see him, and on this night particularly, she really needed the calm, peaceful support his presence always brought.

She could tell by the way he nearly fell through the doorway that he was exhausted, and forced herself to pause before verbally unloading on him. "Hi, honey. Dinner's still hot. Sorry, we started without you."

Peter didn't look up from his plate.

Nate dropped his bag and coat onto the chair by the door and then loosened his tie. "No problem." He traveled around the table, kissing each of them on the top of their heads before sliding into his own chair at the head of the table. "Sorry, I should've texted. I didn't think I'd be that late. I'm glad you started without me." He took a deep breath as he picked up a serving spoon. "Smells delicious. Thanks, Sandy."

"You're welcome. Don't get too excited. It's a little dry."

His eyes traveled around the table. She knew he was looking for gravy, but he was smart enough not to ask for it out loud. "So, how was everyone's day?" he asked, as he mashed his potato with his fork.

Sandra passed him the butter as she sneaked a look at her oldest son. "You go first," she said to Nate. "How was *your* day?"

He shrugged. "About the same as always. Long. Difficult. But worth it." Her husband *really* believed in education, believed he was changing the world for the better, one impossible decision at a time.

Peter's fork clanged against his plate, startling her. She looked at him, and he was staring at his father. "I got in trouble today for pushing Cameron Thompson. I hardly touched him, but he fell down, and they wanted to suspend me, but Mom talked them out of it."

Nate's mouth fell open, his face registering horror.

Sandra could read his mind. The way that Peter had phrased it, this was his worst nightmare. She put a hand on Nate's arm. "Wait a second. It's not as bad as it sounds. Peter was defending some second graders, who Cameron was being *really* mean to. Peter was trying to do a *good* thing." She studied Nate's face. She thought he was relaxing—a little. "Of course, he shouldn't have gotten physical, but overall, I'm quite proud of him."

Nate pulled his eyes away from Peter's face to look at her, his eyebrows arched. "*Proud* of him? He got in trouble for pushing a younger kid to the ground!"

"Yes," she said quickly. "And like I said, it's not a perfect scenario, but his heart was in the right place."

"And what about you?" Nate asked, sounding a smidgen hostile. "How, exactly, did you talk them out of suspension?"

She fought not to roll her eyes. A principal's son getting suspended. Oh, the horror. "Not *them*. Just Mrs. Van DeVenter. And I didn't talk her out of anything. I only stuck up for our son, and she easily saw that it wasn't a situation that warranted suspension."

"And what does it warrant, exactly?"

"May I be excused?" Joanna asked.

Sandra looked at her plate. She'd eaten all the meat, and none of the potatoes or carrots.

"No" and "yes," Nate and Sandra said in unison.

Joanna looked confused.

"Fine," Nate said. "Take one bite of carrot, and then you can go."

Joanna puckered up her face as she slid the world's smallest chunk of root vegetable between her teeth and then ran off before she'd even chewed. Sandra wondered if she'd find that carrot bite in a plant pot later.

Sandra lowered her voice and concentrated on sounding calm and respectful. "It warranted probation."

"Probation?"

"Yes," Sandra said. "He got a warning. Really, honey, it wasn't a big deal."

Nate's eyes slid from hers to Peter's and back to hers. "I'm tired. How about we talk about this later, Peter?"

Fine. Let them duke it out later. This hiccup was the least of her worries.

Peter agreed. "May I be excused too?" He picked up a carrot and shoved it into his mouth. "I ate my carrot," he said through his full mouth.

Sandra smiled. She knew it was the only thing he'd eaten, but Nate didn't know that. Peter would be out of bed digging through the fridge at ten o'clock for another supper. She waited for Nate to answer him, and when he didn't, she said, "Of course."

Peter slinked away toward the stairs, and her heart swelled with affection. She remembered how hard it was to grow up.

She let Nate eat for a few minutes, concentrating on minimizing Sammy's highchair mess, until she couldn't stand it anymore. She put a hand over Nate's. "There's something else."

He let a long exhale out of the side of his mouth. "What?"

"At church. Peter's being bullied at church." Her voice cracked on the words. "Ethan and Jack. They're picking on him—"

He guffawed. This was the *last* reaction she'd expected. "Ethan and Jack? That's crazy! It's probably just boys being boys—"

"No." It was her turn to interrupt. "This is *not* just boys being boys. As an educator, you should know how serious this—"

"Don't tell me how to be an educator, Sandra!"

She leaned back in her chair, not knowing how to proceed. She didn't want to fight with him and hadn't even gotten to the bit about the widow and the angel yet.

"What did he say happened?"

Sandra focused on folding her napkin. "He didn't give specifics."

"So how do you even know anything happened?"

"Because he said so." She took a deep breath. "I didn't want to push, because I didn't want him to clam up. But I know my son, and if he says he's being bullied, he's being bullied." She snapped her mouth shut, suddenly really sick of talking.

Nate slid his chair back with a scraping sound that made Sammy jump and stare in his direction, a smashed carrot frozen halfway to his mouth. Sammy's eyes followed Nate as he walked to the bottom of the stairs.

"Peter!" he hollered up the stairs. "Please come back down here!"

Chapter 13

With dinner abandoned and Sammy scrubbed down and contained in his Pack 'n Play, Peter and his parents settled down on the sectional sofa in the living room. Nate's eyes were puffy with exhaustion, and Sandra had a pang of guilt for making him deal with this right now. Maybe she should have waited for the weekend. Oh well, too late now.

"What's going on at church, son? Talk to us."

Maybe it was having both his parents flanking him, or maybe it was the dim lighting of the living room, but Peter looked more comfortable than he had all day. "Those guys are just trying to make my life miserable."

"How so?" Nate prodded.

Peter tipped his head back and closed his eyes. "They call me names. Call me sissy. Tell everyone not to talk to me." He shrugged, trying to play it cool. Sandra's heart cracked.

"What else?"

"Isn't that enough?" Peter cried. He no longer looked comfortable.

"Peter, I need some specifics if I'm going to take this to their parents—"

"No!" Peter cried, his eyes wide. "You can't! You'll make it so much worse."

Nate grimaced. "I have to. That's how we resolve these things, by *talking* about them. That's what it means to be an adult. And give me some credit. I think I know a little about conflict resolution."

Peter's face made it clear that he did not believe that. Sandra believed that Nate believed it.

"So, specifics," Nate said.

"There aren't any." Peter was done talking.

"So you want me to go to their parents and ask them to make their sons stop calling you a sissy? Don't you think that might prove their point?"

Sandra put her head in her hands. She wanted to support her husband, but he was really butchering this.

"No!" Peter cried. "I don't want you to do anything! Can't we just forget it? I'm sorry I pushed Cameron!" Sandra could tell that he wanted to stomp away, but didn't quite dare to.

"Cameron? What does he have to do with this?"

Peter's eyes welled up with tears. He swallowed hard.

Sandra tried to come to his rescue. "Peter was extra defensive of those second graders because he identified with them. He probably wouldn't have had such a strong reaction to what was happening there if it wasn't for the stuff he's been going through at church. That's all. And how about if we just have Ethan's parents over for coffee? We could just have a discussion. We don't have to give them any specifics. Just a discussion, not a cease and desist."

"Mom!" Peter cried. "You're not helping! And it's not just Ethan. It's all of them."

"I don't really have time to have coffee with these people," Nate said. "I just wanted to say something to them on Sunday and hope they would discipline their own kids." His tone made it clear he didn't want to hear any more of her suggestions. She wasn't even sure that he knew which parents matched with which kids at church, unless they were teenagers who went to his school. Then he knew them.

They sat in silence for a minute, fat tears sliding down Peter's cheeks. Sandra slid closer to him, put her arm around him and squeezed him as hard as she dared. She kissed him on the temple. "I know this is awful, honey, but it is only a season. We're going to get through this."

He let her do all this, but was rigid beneath her touch. "Can I go back to my room now? I'm tired."

Sandra didn't want to let him go.

"Sure," Nate said.

Peter disappeared, leaving them in silence again. Under the circumstances, Sandra decided she'd be better off if she didn't tell her husband about the angel and the widow at this time. Instead, she carried Sammy upstairs, changed him, and then put him in his crib. It was early for sleep yet, but maybe she'd get lucky. Then she went into her bedroom, changed into her pajamas, and spent some time praying for her son. As she silently pleaded his case, she felt a renewed peace settle over her. She also got the undeniable impression that winds of change were about to blow. She could almost feel them on her face already.

Chapter 14

When Sandra got home from dropping the kids off at school, she found Bob sitting on her porch swing. "This is getting to be a habit."

"Can we go inside? You know, the neighbors."

Sandra realized how much she'd missed her new angel friend. "Of course. Come on in." She unlocked the door and then held it open so that he could go in first, spending only a second wondering how this might appear to onlookers. Oh well. There probably weren't very many, if any, onlookers anyway.

She freed Sammy from his car seat, and he squawked in appreciation, not taking his eyes off Bob. "I still can't believe he can see you."

Bob didn't answer. He was too busy making googly eyes at the baby.

"How old are people when they lose that ability?"

All expression fell from Bob's face. "Some things I am not permitted to discuss."

She snorted. "Proprietary information?"

"Huh?" The angel looked flummoxed.

Robin Merrill

"Never mind. Would you like to sit?" Did angels sit down? They did while they were waiting on porch swings. Apparently, they also sat on couches. At least Bob did. He plopped down on the sofa as if he'd been waiting to do just that for a great stretch of eternity. Should she offer him a drink? Did angels drink? *What* did angels drink? Probably not Crystal Light. Certainly not Moxie. Lavender-infused coconut water with gold flecks floating on top? She opened her mouth to hazard a guess, but he didn't give her a chance to offer him anything.

"So, I heard what the ref said to you yesterday when you were talking to Peter's coach."

"You did?" She'd entirely forgotten about that particular revelation. She'd been too busy worrying about Peter. She and Sammy sat down on the ottoman.

"I did. What do you think it means?"

How should she know? He was the one with supernatural powers. "I don't know. But it did occur to me that *that's* what Mr. Fenton was talking about. Maybe he didn't mean the *team* white. Maybe he meant the *man* White. But it still doesn't make perfect sense, because he did say, 'You have to stop *them.* You have to stop *white.*' I don't know." She really didn't.

"I think he meant White, the man." Bob sounded gravely serious.

"Why? What do you know that I don't know?"

"I don't know anything, but the man was *murdered.* I don't think his last words would have been about a middle school soccer team, no matter how rough they were playing. I think it makes sense that his last words would be about naming his killer."

"He didn't say that White was his killer. He said I had to stop them. So who is *them*? And where *were* you? You were there eavesdropping? Is that really how it works?"

He looked offended. "It's not eavesdropping."

"Sorry," she said and meant it. She hadn't meant it as an affront. She was truly curious.

"We need a plan." If his feelings had been hurt, he'd recovered quickly.

She laughed. "A plan? What kind of plan?" She couldn't imagine a plan that she could be a part of.

He pointed at her. "You need to go undercover."

"What?" *This angel is insane.* Undercover as what, a middle school soccer player?

He nodded dramatically. "I mean it. I happen to know that this region is *absolutely desperate* for soccer officials."

She paused, speechless. "You're kidding."

He shook his head, slowly, dramatically. "I am not."

"I hardly know the rules."

"That is true of several middle school soccer officials."

She wasn't considering it. She was just having trouble coming up with excuses. "I am far too busy. I would miss Peter's games."

"They could schedule your games around his. He doesn't play every day. I'm telling you—you only have to do one game a week and you'll be on the inside. You'll get the scoop."

"Can't *you* get the scoop? Can't you eavesdrop on the refs when they're talking to each other?"

"I told you that I can't always do that. I can't just go everywhere I please, and I can't be everywhere at once. It's complicated. Plus, it's not like I have a lot of spare time on my hands."

"And I do?" she cried. "Do you know anything about my life? I don't have a single second of downtime!" Right on cue, Sammy began to bellow. She kissed him on his chubby cheek and then set him on the floor. She pushed a few toys in front of him and then returned to the angel. "Is this request coming from you or from God?"

He looked sad. "Just from me. But I could really use your help. I'll continue to investigate, but if you could join me, we'd be faster."

She smirked. "Investigate? Are you some sort of angel sleuth?"

"No. Never been in this sort of predicament before. I just want to make up for my blunder, and then I'll stop with the sleuthing. Believe me, I don't enjoy it."

A knock sounded on her front door. She looked at Bob in a panic, as if she expected him to hide.

"I'll leave if you want me to, but whoever it is won't be able to see me."

"Unless it's an infant knocking on the door."

She couldn't be sure, but she thought she heard Sammy giggle at that.

"Right. Unless it's an infant. And I can even hide myself from them when I need to."

She headed for the door, wondering under what circumstances an angel would ever need to hide himself from an infant. She peeked through the peephole and gasped. She looked at Bob. "It's the widow!" she whispered, too loudly.

"Okay!" he whispered back. "Open the door!" He didn't even pretend to be surprised. He'd known who it was before she'd told him, she was sure of it. That was annoying.

She swung the door open and put on her best Sunday morning smile. "Hi, Isabelle! What a lovely surprise!"

Chapter 15

"You're probably wondering how I know where you live," Isabelle said, her voice deep and strained, as if it had taken a lot of gumption to push those words out.

Nope. It hadn't occurred to Sandra to wonder such a thing. Showed how ill-equipped she was to be a secret sleuth. But now that Isabelle had mentioned it, Sandra *was* curious. Yet before she could demand a confession, Isabelle offered one.

"I followed you home yesterday." She studied the toes of her own shoes.

Under the circumstances, Sandra didn't find such a thing all that strange. She stepped back. "Would you like to come in?" Sandra cast her eyes to the couch, thinking Bob had probably vanished, but he still sat there staring at the scene unfolding before him.

Isabelle stepped inside. "Thank you. I'm sorry, but I thought it was weird that you stopped by yesterday. So I followed you to try to figure out who you were. But you just drove home and got out of a minivan, just an ordinary mom." Isabelle's eyes scanned the place behind her as if the sight of Sandra's home confirmed her ordinariness.

"Yep, just an ordinary mom." *Who happens to talk to angels.* "Would you like to have a seat?"

For one scary second, it appeared Isabelle was going to sit squarely on Bob's lap, but he moved just in time. Though, he didn't exactly slide down the couch. He just vanished and then reappeared two feet away, his disappearance and reappearance seeming to happen simultaneously. It was the strangest thing Sandra had ever seen.

"Are you all right?" Isabelle asked, and Sandra realized she was frowning and staring at what to Isabelle appeared to be an empty spot on the couch.

"Yes, sorry. I guess I'm still a bit shook up by all this." Sandra looked at Sammy to make sure he was still where she'd left him. He was, so she returned to her ottoman. "What can I do for you?"

She took a shaky breath. "I didn't know where else to go. My friends all … well, I don't have very many friends, and those I do have, well …" She was having great difficulties. "They just might turn on me. Or maybe they already …"

She stared intently at Sandra. "I have no idea if I can trust you, but yesterday, it seemed like you knew more than you said you did, you know, by mentioning Mike."

It took Sandra a second to remember who Mike was, and then she looked at Bob wide-eyed. So this *was* about a man named White!

Isabelle's eyes followed Sandra's to the empty seat beside her, and she frowned. "What are you looking at?"

"Sorry." Sandra jerked her eyes away from the angel, who wasn't being much help anyway. He looked as bewildered as she felt. "I was just thinking." She loved that Isabelle thought she had some sort of inside scoop. She shouldn't say much, or that illusion would be shattered.

"So, you can imagine that I can't exactly go to the cops."

Wow! This *was* juicy! "Right," Sandra said slowly, because she didn't know what else to say.

"Oh, shoot. I'm not making any sense." Isabelle put her head in her hands. "I didn't even tell you about the break-in," she said through her fingers.

"What break-in?" Sandra spurred her on because Isabelle appeared to be done with the conversation.

"Last night. I was out." She picked up her head and looked at Sandra, and her cheeks were red. "And while I was out, *someone*, probably White or his goons, went through my house. They trashed the place."

Huh. Puzzle pieces. Lots of 'em. And Sandra had no clue what to do with them. She wanted *so badly* to look at Bob for help. She had no idea what to say next.

She took the leap. "And why do you think this was Mike?"

Isabelle looked at Sandra as if appalled at her stupidity. "Because my husband named him with his dying breath! To a *stranger*!"

Oh yeah. That. "What do you think they were looking for?"

Isabelle shrugged. "I was hoping you'd know."

Sandra fought back a laugh. That was rich. Isabelle was seriously overestimating her knowledge of this situation. She tried to make her face impassive. Maybe she did know, maybe she didn't.

Bob started waving at her, his eyes wide and wild. She shook her head slightly. She didn't want to get caught looking at him again. He pointed at the door. Oh! It was a game of charades!

"Maybe we should go take a look," she blurted out, like a wild guess in a game of Pictionary when the time's running out.

Isabelle nodded. "I knew you'd say that."

She had? Sandra hadn't even known she'd say that! "Okay, let's go." Then she remembered Sammy. "Actually, give me a minute. I can't take the baby." She chewed on her lip. She didn't really want to invite the *Pretty Little Liars* girl back over. She looked back to Isabelle. "Let me find a sitter. Then I'll meet you there."

Isabelle frowned, as if she didn't believe Sandra.

"I promise. I'll be right there."

Chapter 16

Sandra looked at Bob, wild-eyed. "I can't take the baby with me! What am I going to do?"

Bob nodded emphatically, obviously itching to go inspect the break-in himself. "Hang on. I have an idea." And then he was gone.

Sandra groaned. Would that ever stop being annoying? She stooped to pick up Sammy and checked his diaper. Sure enough, it was in need of attention. He grinned wildly at her as she stripped him down, as if he enjoyed having a mommy-servant to attend to his every need.

Bob reappeared before she'd finished buttoning Sammy's overalls.

"That was quick."

"I *am* an angel of the Lord."

"So you keep reminding me." She scooped Sammy off the table and squared herself to Bob. "So, is there a plan?"

"What do you think of Ethel Baxter?"

Ethel Baxter? She didn't think anything of her. She knew the name. Ethel was one of the many older women who sat in the back of her church, but she didn't think she could pick her out of a police lineup. Still, she was embarrassed to admit to an angel that she didn't know the people in her own church. "I don't really think anything," she said. *Lame.*

"Well, I have it on good authority that she is just *dying* to babysit."

She was? Seriously? "How much does she cost?"

He shrugged. "I don't think she'd charge anything, but if she did, it wouldn't be much. Besides, today you might not have much cash, but when you're reffing, you'll get paid and you'll be able to give her a cut—"

"I never said I was going to become a ref, Bob. That's insane."

"You *did* say that, though."

Had she? She really didn't think so.

"And either way, you need her now, so give her a call."

Sandra narrowed her eyes at him. "How do you know she wants to babysit?"

He shrugged again. "I asked your church angel."

She felt her eyes grow wide. "We have a church angel?"

"Of course you do!"

This new tidbit of knowledge elated her. If she'd thought about it, she might have assumed such a thing, but she didn't think she'd ever thought about it. Sure, she knew there were angels around, but the fact that one was *assigned* to her church—how cool was that? The angels were so organized! She looked around her messy living room and hoped Bob wasn't offended by the chaos.

"So ... call her!" Bob shifted his weight from his right to his left foot and back again. It appeared he had to go to the bathroom. Did angels even go to the bathroom? She didn't think so.

"Okay," she agreed without really agreeing. She was just going to call Ethel out of the blue and ask her to babysit? She'd never even spoken to the woman. That would be so rude. "I can't," she squeaked out meekly.

"Of course you can." He lowered his head and sighed. "Just dial the number."

"No, I mean ... what am I going to say?"

"You're going to say that you heard she might be interested in babysitting."

Sammy squirmed in her arms as if he was tired of the debate. "And what if she asks me where I heard it?"

He smirked. "You don't want to tell her that the angels told you?"

She did her best to glare at him.

"She won't ask. Just call. Where's your church directory?"

How did he know she had a church directory? Sometimes he was creepy. Or maybe everyone had a church directory. She went into the kitchen, to the giant drawer in the corner that they had deemed "the junk drawer" and pulled it open with one trembling hand. Why was she so nervous to do this? This was crazy. She was going to go "investigate" a crime scene, but she was terrified to call a sister in Christ? She dug through the drawer with one hand, taking care not to slice her hand open on some forgotten, hidden sharp object. At first, she thought the directory wasn't in there, but then, beneath the rubber bands, stripped screws, mystery keys, used birthday candles, old phone chargers, and yellowed appliance manuals, she found it. She pulled it out, and a pair of dog nail clippers came with it. They didn't even own a dog. She slid them back into the drawer. They might get a dog one day. She shut the drawer and looked at Bob sheepishly. "We don't use this much."

He nodded, as if he'd heard that before.

She took a deep breath. She would never do this, never *be able* to do this if there wasn't an angel standing in her kitchen staring at her.

Ethel answered on the third ring.

Sandra gulped. "Hi, is this Ethel?"

"It is." She sounded cheery enough.

"Hi, Ethel. This is Sandra Provost, from church? I sit on the other side from you, about five rows up—"

"Yes, dear. I know who you are."

"Oh great." She swallowed, her mouth suddenly bone-dry. "I'm calling because … well, feel free to say no … but I was wondering …"

Bob widened his eyes at her, telepathically communicating *Get to the point.*

"Well … I heard you like to babysit." She spat the last few words out and instantly regretted it. This was so ridiculous.

"Oh!" Ethel cried. "I do! I do like to babysit! My kids are all grown and gone, and no matter how much I beg, they haven't given me any grandbabies yet!"

Sandra exhaled rapidly. To Ethel, it had probably sounded as if Sandra had blown into her ear. "Oh wow, that's so great. I just need some help with my little one, Sammy. He's still only—"

"Yes, yes, I've seen you toting him around. When you do need me?"

She gulped. This part was also absurd. "Right now? I need to take care of something, and I don't think he'd enjoy it."

"Of course, of course!" Ethel was as eager and enthusiastic as a Grace Space saleswoman.

Maybe she *was* a Grace Space saleswoman? A current of fear struck Sandra's gut. Oh well, even if she was, this would be worth it. She was just itching to catch up to Isabelle. If that meant buying an eighteen-dollar lip balm, then so be it.

"Do you know where I live?"

Sandra's shame deepened. Of course she didn't know where Ethel lived.

Ethel didn't wait for a response. She just began giving her convoluted directions. Sandra closed her eyes to try to focus, but she quickly lost track of the landmarks. "Actually, can you just give me your address? I'll use my GPS."

Chapter 17

A wet-faced Isabelle opened her front door, and Sandra stepped inside. Isabelle slammed the door in Bob's face, but he appeared inside anyway, and his mouth instantly fell open.

Sandra followed his gaze to Isabelle's large living room and sure enough, it was a gawk-worthy sight. "Are you sure they were looking for something? Maybe they were just *trying* to trash the place."

Isabelle walked over to a set of drawers that had been pulled out and tipped over. She pushed one of them with her toe. "I'm pretty sure they were looking for something."

Sandra gingerly walked into the room, taking care where she stepped. There wasn't much open floor. They'd pulled the cushions off the furniture and cut into every one of them. Stuffing spilled out in all directions, hiding broken glass from tossed picture frames. Books had been opened, rifled through, and dropped with the spines facing up. Whoever had done this—they were animals. "Your husband must have been quite the reader." As soon as the words left her lips, she regretted them. She'd assumed, based on the fact that Isabelle was beautiful and wore nice shoes that she couldn't be the reader in the house.

But Isabelle didn't seem to notice the slight. "He was a teacher. He loved books."

Sandra stooped to pick one of the many books up, closed it, and looked at the cover. *A Framework for Understanding Poverty.* She looked around the room. "I'm guessing Frank didn't know much about poverty himself?"

Sandra felt Bob wince, even though he was six feet away. This time, Isabelle *was* offended. "Frank worked hard all his life. Don't assume he was a rich snob. He loved his students, gave his whole life for them."

Sandra gave the room another glance. She knew what she wanted to ask. But did she dare? "Isabelle? This looks like a really nice place for a teacher's salary." She was going to also ask, "Where did Frank get his cash?" but Isabelle anticipated the question and answered it.

"Frank comes from money." She held out both hands. "He inherited it. He didn't have to be a teacher to pay the bills. He *chose* to be a teacher because he loved kids and wanted to make the world a better place."

In an instant, Sandra's heart softened toward this woman. Sandra was married to a younger version of the same man—only without the wealth. "I'm so sorry he's gone, Isabelle. He sounds like an awesome person." *And he* doesn't *sound like a criminal.*

Isabelle's tears started falling again, and she swiped at them with the back of a hand. "He sure was." She wiped her nose on her sleeve and then added with a creaky voice, "And before you ask, I'll tell you that he left everything to his own children. He left me enough to get by, but I won't be rich or anything."

At first, Sandra had no idea why Isabelle had just shared this detail. Then it dawned on her. "Oh, no, Isabelle, I wasn't going to accuse you of anything. You're obviously grieving over your loss of him. I would never assume you had anything to do with it." *Unless you're the world's best actress.* She was pretty enough to be an actress.

Sandra looked around the room, wondering what to look for. What would Monk notice? Or

Father Brown? Or that cutie pie from *Psych*? She wished she'd paid more attention to those shows. If Frank Fenton was already rich, then he didn't need a secret life of crime, right? Or maybe he *was* involved in a secret life of crime just for the thrills? Or maybe he wasn't as rich as Isabelle thought he was? "Do you have access to Frank's bank statements?" she asked before thinking about the question. She thought she heard Bob gasp, but he was over on the other side of the room, inspecting some ripped up paintings.

"I guess. Why?" Her voice had tightened.

Sandra had trouble holding her words back long enough to consider them. She wanted to see those bank statements so badly that her chest was burning. "I just want to see if Frank really had the money you think he did."

She scowled. "Of course he did. But if you need to see them, I guess ..." She turned to go into the kitchen, and Sandra followed. The kitchen was in even more of a mess than the living room. Drawers dumped and flipped over, chairs overturned, stove and fridge torn apart. What could they possibly have been looking for? Isabelle went straight through the kitchen and into another room, which turned out to be an office with an even bigger collection of books on the floor. *This must have taken them forever.* Isabelle stooped to rifle through some papers and came up with a single page of an open bank statement.

The single page was enough. It showed a running balance, and the balance was huge. Sandra quickly handed it back to her. "You're right. That's a lot of zeros. I'm sorry I doubted you."

"It's okay."

Her ready agreement raised a question in Sandra's mind. Why did Isabelle want her here? Why did she seem to want her help? "Isabelle? If Frank wasn't doing anything illegal, then why can't you call the police?"

Isabelle looked at her as if she were stupid. "I thought you knew about Mike."

"I do," Sandra tried to recover, "but Frank was innocent, right?"

Isabelle nodded, but she didn't look so sure. "I think so."

"What does that mean?"

"I mean …" She averted Sandra's gaze. Bob appeared beside Sandra then, looking eager as ever. "I mean that I don't exactly know *what* Mike and those guys are up to. I just know that it's something shady. Suddenly, they wouldn't talk to Frank anymore, and their wives wouldn't talk to me. We were all friends, and then just, *boom*. Something changed, only a few days ago. I asked Frank about it, but he just told me not to worry. And he didn't seem worried, so I *didn't* worry. But now it sure seems there was something to worry about, doesn't there?" The more she talked, the faster the words spilled out. She fell into the office chair, which was, Sandra was grateful, upright, and put her face in her hands. "And I guess I'm just *scared* of them!"

Sandra stepped closer to her and put her hand on her shoulder. "But, Isabelle, if you're in danger, the police can protect you better than an ordinary mom in a minivan can."

Isabelle sniffed and looked up at Sandra with wet eyes. "But what if Frank *was* involved? They were all such good pals. What if Frank was involved with whatever it was and then something went wrong? I just don't know!"

This doesn't make any sense. "Why would you think Frank might have been involved?"

"Because they were all such good *friends,*" she spat out, making sure the word *friends* spun with a healthy dose of irony. "If they were doing something wrong, surely Frank knew about it, and if he knew about it, why didn't he tell anyone? Trust me. I've been trying to figure this out. My husband was *murdered.* I've thought about nothing else. But no matter how much I think, I can't figure it out. But one thing's for sure, if he *was* mixed up in something shady, *I'm* not going to be the one to expose him. I'd rather go on not knowing what happened to him or why it happened than to ruin his reputation. He doesn't deserve that, no matter what."

Chapter 18

Ethel lived in the downstairs apartment of a giant, old house. From the outside, the place didn't stand out from the long row of other old houses on the quiet side street. But when Sandra stepped inside, for the second time that day, she was enveloped in an invisible welcome hug. Soft music played in the distance, and the brightly colored, well-lit space smelled of fresh bread and cinnamon. When Ethel offered her a cup of tea, she almost burst into tears at the sweetness of it all.

Yet, she asked for a rain check on the tea. Though she had nowhere to rush off to, her brain was rushing around in her head, and she wanted to be alone. Or, as close to alone as one could be with a baby and a new best friend angel.

Ethel graciously granted the rain check and then just as graciously declined the paltry stack of dollar bills Sandra held out to her. "Are you kidding?" she chirped. "I should be paying you for this treat! Little Sammy has been the highlight of my whole week!"

"Do you ever work in the church nursery?" Sandra asked as she tried to wrestle Sammy into his car seat. He was almost too big for it. She groaned at the thought of upgrading. Maybe she *should* ref a few soccer games, if only for the few extra dollars.

"I'm on the list, and they know I'm available if they need me, but I so hate to miss the sermon, and the young moms like to hang out in there and chitchat during the service, and I wouldn't want to interfere with that. I remember how lonely it can be being home with the baby all week long." She gave Sandra an encouraging smile. "But if you *ever* need help with any of your kiddos, I'll be right here. I don't get out much."

Sandra decided then and there that she and her kids had to take Ethel somewhere. Out to lunch, or to the beach when the weather got nice again. She slid the car seat off the table. "Thanks, Ethel, you're the best." She had the urge to hug the woman, but she was on the other side of the table, and Sandra didn't want to make things awkward. She'd never hugged the woman before. Maybe she'd shoot for a

Sunday hug, when everybody was already in the mood.

"You bet." She gave a little wave to Sammy. "You have a good rest of your day."

Sandra returned to her car to find Bob in the front seat. She tucked Sammy into the back and then slid behind the wheel. She put the keys in the ignition, but then she just sat there. "Now what?"

"I'm not sure."

She looked at him. How could he not have a plan? He was a supernatural being. She put the car in reverse and slid out of the driveway.

"Maybe you could go help Isabelle clean up?"

Oh sure, volunteer *her* for the heavy labor. "I offered."

"You did?" He sounded shocked. "Sorry, I didn't hear you."

She bit back a retort about his eavesdropping prowess. "She didn't want my help. I'm wondering why she wanted us over there at all. Well, wanted *me* over there. I guess she didn't know you were there. She's obviously suspicious of Frank, yet she was willing to let us snoop around, looking for evidence against him?"

"I don't think she's suspicious of him at all. I think she wanted us to find something that cleared his name. Though I can't imagine what that would be, and we certainly didn't find anything."

"Hard to find something when you don't know what you're looking for."

His head snapped toward her as if a light bulb had popped on. "I guess it's time to find out how to become a soccer official, then."

She snorted. "Oh, is it?"

Each time the idea surfaced, it sounded less terrible. But why? Why was she even considering it? It was preposterous.

You know why you're considering it, a tiny voice in her head said.

Oh, I do? Why?

Because you're bored.

She gasped.

"What is it?"

"Nothing. Just had a thought." Was she bored? Yes, she kind of was. But how was that possible? She was beyond busy and always exhausted. She had a great life and should be content with it. Yet, that annoying, critical voice had a point. She *was* a little bored. Not all the time. But more than once in a while. "I can't do anything without checking with Nate."

"Good. Check with Nate. I've got to go. There's a cross-country meet." He vanished before she could say good-bye.

She said it anyway, to the empty seat beside her. She had more than an hour before she had to pick up the kids from school. It was kind of pointless to go home and unpack Sammy just to pack him up again. Maybe she should go surprise Nate at his school. Just pop in and say hello. Yeah, that was a great idea! She never did that.

The more she thought about it, the more excited she was about the idea. Seeing Sammy in the middle of his workday would surely brighten it. She went through the Dunkin' drive through too, just in case Sammy's sweetness wasn't enough to warrant a surprise visit. Sure, she knew Nate loved his son, but he also really loved vanilla frosted donuts with sprinkles. She bought him two, and ate one on the way.

Chapter 19

Nate wasn't in his office, but his secretary, warily eyeing the baby bucket and the Dunkin' bag, buzzed him through the intercom. Then she granted Sandra a fake smile and said, "He'll be here shortly," even though she knew no such thing. Nate did not come running when his presence was requested.

Sandra turned to go into his office.

"You can wait out here," the secretary said quickly.

Sandra was annoyed, but she did as she was told, and plopped herself down in the small waiting area. At least this one had chairs, unlike the hard bench at her son's school. How had she managed to end up waiting outside the principal's office two days in a row?

As she expected, it was a long wait, but Sammy was in a good mood, so Sandra could fiddle with her phone to pass the time. Then, just when she thought she'd have to leave to go pick up Peter and Joanna, Nate sailed through the door, and indeed, his face did light up at the sight of his family, even before he saw the donut bag. Still, Sandra thought she'd go for the gold and held it up. "Brought you a treat!"

"You're the best!" he cried and bent to kiss her on the cheek. "Come on into my office. You didn't have to wait out here!" He picked up Sammy and then put his hand to the small of her back, a gesture that still gave her the shivers after all these years. As she passed, she flashed a triumphant smile at the secretary, who pretended not to see it.

Once they were settled in his office with the door shut, Nate asked, "So, to what do I owe the pleasure?"

"We just wanted to pop in and say hi."

He tilted his head and narrowed his eyes. "I don't believe that for a second."

She giggled. "Well, I *did* want to ask you something."

"Shoot. Anything for you." He shuffled some papers around on his desk, already distracted.

For once, she didn't mind. It might be good if he was a little distracted for this question. She took a deep breath. "I know this sounds like it's coming out of left field, but I've actually been thinking about it for a few days."

He nodded without looking up. He was staring at a spreadsheet.

"I was thinking about becoming a soccer official."

That got his attention. His face snapped up and his lips parted a little. Then he just stared at her.

She held up a hand. "Hear me out. I've learned that they are desperate for officials, and I think it would be fun—"

"Do you even know the rules?"

"They will teach me the rules."

He frowned. "I'm not so sure that's true."

"Well, then, I'll learn them myself. That's why God made YouTube. It's not a very complicated game."

"Right, but there are lots of little rules that only refs know. Do you know how far back a kid's allowed to stand before kicking a corner kick?"

She tried not to let it show on her face, but she was pretty sure there was no rule regarding that question. "I'm an intelligent woman, Nate. I can learn the rules to a simple sport."

It was his turn to hold up a hand. "Don't get defensive. This is the first I'm hearing of this, so give me a chance to process." He folded his hands on his desk and leveled a gaze at her. It appeared he was trying to think up arguments.

"I just don't get it," he finally said. "Do you even *like* soccer?"

She didn't. Not really. She liked that Peter liked soccer. "Of course I like soccer. And it would bring in some extra money—" As soon as the words left her lips, she wished they hadn't.

He flinched. "We don't need you to work, Sandra."

"I know that. But there's no such thing as too much money, and I could use the exercise." She couldn't give two hoots about exercise, but the more he resisted, the more she wanted to make this happen.

"How are you going to have time?"

"I will only take games that don't conflict with Peter's schedule, and I found a free babysitter."

His eyes grew wide. Finally, some news he liked. "Free? Who?"

"Ethel Baxter." She was certain he wouldn't know who that was.

"Oh, Ethel?" he cried. "She's a lovely lady!"

I stand corrected. "She sure is. And she just loves Sammy."

"She does? How do you know that?"

Oops. How was she supposed to explain why she'd dropped off their son in the middle of the day so she could go all secret super sleuth at a widow's house? "I … I went over to a friend's house today. Her house was broken into, and she needed some help picking up." Not *exactly* a lie. Probably too close to a lie to qualify as truth, but her conscience only piped up a little.

"Really? How lovely of you. What friend?"

"Isabelle."

"Isabelle?" He scowled. "I don't remember you mentioning an Isabelle."

This was getting so sticky. Best to redirect. "I really want to do this. At least try it. If it causes a lot of problems for the family, of course I'll stop." She knew that it wouldn't cause any problems.

He chewed on his lip. "I *guess* so."

Really? That was easier than she'd expected. "Thanks, Nate!"

"Sure. Do you have any idea how to become a soccer ref?"

She shook her head. "None."

He gave her a patronizing smirk.

"It can't be that hard to figure out, Nate. I can just Google it."

He picked up his phone. "Let me make a call. I know the guy in charge of the local district of soccer referees." He punched some numbers and then waited. Then he said, in his official professional voice, "Could I speak to Mike White, please?"

Chapter 20

Sandra greeted her two oldest children as they climbed into the van, but she was operating in rote mode. Only when some part of her consciousness noticed the sullen look on Peter's face did she snap into the moment. "What's wrong, honey?"

He tried to ignore her.

She didn't let him. She knew how to pester someone. She'd learned it from him.

"I'm just anxious about practice."

She took a moment to be proud of her son's self-awareness and then asked, "Why are you worried about practice?"

"I think Coach is still mad at me." He didn't say it outright, but she thought she heard some accusation in his tone—as if he was also saying, "You made things worse by hollering at my coach."

"Well, he shouldn't be," she said. *Lame.* That was the best she could do?

"I apologized to Cameron."

She looked at Peter, stunned. He did? "You did?" No one had told him to do that!

"I told him I was sorry for pushing him, but that he still shouldn't be picking on people."

Sandra thought that over. "So you apologized and then implied a threat before walking away."

Peter actually chuckled, and Sandra had a heady moment. It was so rare that she was able to make her son laugh. "Yeah, I guess so."

They rode the rest of the way home in silence, as Sandra analyzed Peter's church situation. Wasn't there something she could do? Maybe Bob could help. He was, after all, the local middle school sports angel. Couldn't he intervene? If not, what good was having friends in high places?

She'd just pulled into their driveway when her cell rang. She didn't recognize the number, so she ignored it. "Can you get Sammy, Peter?"

He grunted his assent, and she walked to her house with only a diaper bag and a purse, feeling light as a feather. Her eyes lingered on her porch swing as she walked by, as if willing Bob to appear. Did she miss him? She'd have to put that swing away soon. Winter was coming. A sharp breeze blew some leaves across her lawn as if Mother Nature was agreeing with her.

Peter followed her into the house, swinging Sammy from his taut arm like a wild pendulum.

"Easy!" she cried. "He'll throw up!" She didn't think this was likely, but she was grateful to her son for toting the car seat around, so she tried to soften her correction with language her fifth-grader would appreciate.

Peter plopped the seat down on the couch, sat down beside Sammy, and began to unbuckle him. This was a bonus. Usually, he just left him on the floor, strapped in, at the mercy of Mr. T. "I'm starving," Peter said.

"I know you are. I'll get some snacks out."

She didn't see Peter roll his eyes, but she could hear it in his voice. "Baby carrots don't count as a snack."

"Want me to make some dip?" she called out without turning around.

"Yes, please!" Wow, she'd even gotten a please.

Joanna scrambled up onto one of the kitchen chairs. "I love baby carrots."

Sandra bent to kiss her on the top of the head. "I know you do, sweetie." She straightened up and went to the fridge, where she retrieved the bag of carrots. She opened them and put them on the table, before turning back to gather dip ingredients. Peter strapped Sammy into his high chair.

"Thanks for being so helpful!"

Peter looked down, his cheeks flushed, so she stopped praising him.

Her phone rang again, and she checked to see who was calling. Was that the same number that had called five minutes ago? She thought so, but she wasn't sure. She almost answered it, but decided not to. Then, when it stopped ringing, she checked the call history, and sure enough, it was the same number. *I might not be Sherlock, but I'm capable of some smart phone sleuthing.* She copied and pasted the number into a search engine, then waited impatiently for results.

"Mom," Peter said, making the word four syllables long, "the dip?"

"Just a sec," she said without looking up.

The search came back void, and she gave up, dropping her phone on the counter and grabbing the sour cream. She had a weird feeling in her stomach. She found herself *really* wishing she'd answered the phone. Who calls twice in five minutes? It must have been important. Maybe she should call the number back. But how disappointed she would be with herself to learn it was a political poll. How many times had she answered the call about the bear baiting bill? Again, she wished Bob were there. Maybe he had supernatural caller identification ability.

She licked some stray sour cream off her finger and then stirred the dip. Then she set it down in front of her kids, two of whom dove for it as though they'd never seen food before. "Can I have some juice?" Peter asked.

She nodded. "You know where it is." She didn't look at him. He was ten. He could get his own juice, which he did. He even offered Joanna some.

Sandra bit back the praise. She checked the clock and realized they didn't have much time to dillydally. "Wheels up in thirty."

Joanna groaned. "We just got home. Where do we have to go?"

"Soccer practice. Sorry, kiddo."

"Do we have to watch?"

Often they just dropped Peter off and ran errands, but this time, Sandra wanted to stay nearby, just in case. In case of what, she wasn't sure, but her mother's intuition was telling her not to go too far from the field. "I would like to watch today, yes."

Peter gave her an annoyed look, but there was just a hint of relief there too.

Chapter 21

Sandra and her two youngest children sat nestled in their minivan, watching Peter's practice. Joanna was zombified by her tablet, Sammy was asleep, and Sandra was considering following his lead when her phone buzzed. This time, she was certain it was the same number, and curiosity got the best of her. She answered on the second ring. If it was a political poll, she would suffer the consequences.

"Hello?"

"Hello. Is this Sandra Provost?"

"It is."

"Hi, Sandra. This is Mike White calling …"

Sandra's entire body went cold.

"What's wrong, Mama?" Joanna asked from beside her.

"I'm the president of the local SOOM district … Ms. Provost? Are you there?"

Sandra gulped. Her throat felt as though it had just swallowed a sandy camel. "I'm here."

"Great. Your husband said you were interested in becoming a soccer official?" His words began to spill out faster, as if he had more pressing matters to attend to and had to speed up this tiresome conversation. Maybe he had someone else to murder. Or maybe the man just had to go to the bathroom. "Can you attend some training tonight?"

Tonight? She didn't respond immediately.

He wasn't a patient man. "Does tonight work? If it does, we could have you on the field by Saturday."

"What's wrong, Mama?" Joanna asked again.

Sandra put a hand on her leg, trying to ease her panic, but that hand was trembling, and Joanna's eyes grew even wider.

Sandra was frozen with panic. Yes, she may well be talking to a murderer on the phone, but that wasn't even on the fear radar right now. *On the field by Saturday?* That was nuts! This whole thing was nuts! She never should have taken this path. She should have stuck to her blessedly simple mom routine, even if it was a little redundant. She opened her mouth to tell Mr. Murdering Mike White that she had changed her mind, but "Tonight. Sure." came out instead. She squeezed her eyes shut.

"Great! Do you know where White Funeral Home is?"

Her heart pounded so hard it hurt. Was she having a heart attack? Yes, she thought she was. She, a middle-aged soccer mom, was going to die of a heart attack in her minivan. What a cliché!

"It's on Kirkland Street." His voice was gritty with impatience.

"What time?" she managed to squeak out.

"Seven o'clock." He wasn't asking if that was okay with her.

"Great. Thank you." She hung up the phone with a trembling hand and then stared at it as if she'd never seen it before.

"Mama?"

Sandra realized she was now squeezing her daughter's knee. She forced her hand to relax, and forced herself to exhale. *I can do this*, she told herself silently. *It's not a big deal. I'm just going to go meet a murderer at a funeral home, which, conveniently, he seems to own.* No, this was crazy. She could *not* do this. She looked in her rearview, hoping to see Bob in the backseat. Of course, he wasn't there. Angels were never visible when you really needed them. "Bob?" she said aloud, and Joanna scowled at her.

"Who's Bob?"

An insane giggle bubbled up out of Sandra's torso and escaped through her mouth. She was pretty sure she'd never laughed like that. Like an attention-seeking hyena with an especially high-pitched voice. The thought of the hyena made her laugh again, and now Joanna looked on the verge of tears. Sandra sent up a silent prayer, "Lord, help me get a grip." Then she looked down at her daughter's upturned face. Choking back another insane giggle, she caressed her cheek. "I'm sorry, punkin. Didn't mean to scare you. I've just got some adult stuff going on. Nothing for you to worry about."

Joanna didn't look convinced, but she did turn her attention back to her tablet, so Sandra took that as a win. She took another deep breath, and her chest shook, threatening another giggle, so she tried to clear her brain of anything that might set her off again. Then she called her husband.

He didn't answer, as she expected. This was a busy time of day for him. She left him a message, telling him that she would be going for soccer ref training that night at seven. Her voice only cracked twice during the five-second message, but she managed to avoid the lunatic laughter.

With her call finished, she closed her eyes and leaned her head back. *It's okay. I can always back out. I have hours to decide whether or not to actually show up, and whether or not to actually be a soccer ref.* She needed to talk to Bob. More than talk to him. She needed him to go with her. *God,* she prayed, *if Bob's not busy with some golf scuffle, could you send him my way?* Then she opened her eyes and forced herself to focus on Peter's soccer practice.

Not twenty seconds later, Bob appeared beside her window. Her body jerked so hard that the whole van shook. Joanna had gone back to her tablet and didn't look up. Sandra stabbed at the window button, but nothing happened. She hurriedly turned the key in the ignition, scared to death he was going to vanish before she got to talk to him, and then rolled down the window. "Where have you been?" she said, a little surprised by how demanding she sounded.

He looked amused. "Do you really want to have this conversation out loud right here?" He glanced pointedly at Joanna, who remained oblivious.

"Well, you said you can't read my mind!" How else could they have the conversation if not out loud?

"What?" Joanna asked, but didn't look up.

Sandra sighed. "Nothing, honey." She rolled the window up, turned the battery off, and got out of the car. At first, she thought Bob had vanished again, but then she realized he was standing behind the van. She followed him into the shade of an orange-leaved oak tree. Between the shade and the van, they were hidden from view of everyone there. She felt as though she were about to engage in a playground drug deal. She looked at Bob expectantly.

"You beckoned?"

"Wow, that actually works?"

He furrowed his brow. "What works?"

"I prayed and asked for you, and you came. I didn't think that would work."

"Of course it worked. Now, what do you need?" He sounded almost as impatient as Mike had on the phone.

"Mike White called me."

Bob gasped and stepped closer, like a high school cheerleader eager to devour the juiciest tidbit of gossip.

Sandra laughed. She was growing quite fond of—and comfortable with—this supernatural being.

"What?" Bob pushed. "Why did he call you?"

"Well, if you'd check in, *ever*, you'd know that Nate called him last night to ask—"

"Your husband knows him?"

"I guess. Nate knows everyone. Anyway, he asked Mike to get me into reffing. And Mike just called me to tell me that there's training tonight at seven. *At his funeral home.*" She waited for the absurdity, and possible danger, of this last detail to sink in.

"*His* funeral home?" Bob looked perplexed.

She shrugged. "I dunno. He called it White Funeral Home. His name is Mike White. I just put two and two—"

"Well, find out for sure tonight."

"Bob, you have to come with me."

He scrunched up his nose and looked at the sky. Sandra imagined him doing a quick scan of his angelic version of a calendar app. "Sure. Okay."

She breathed out a rush of air. "Awesome. Thank you. But don't be late. I'm not going in without you." She looked him up and down. "If anything should, uh … go wrong … can you defend me?"

"What? What's that supposed to mean?"

"I mean, if he tries to murder me and stuff me in a coffin, can you whip out some miracle power and save me?"

"Of course." His expression, which was completely sans confidence, did not match his words.

"Are you sure?"

"Yes, I'm sure! Stop worrying. He's not going to try to kill you. He has no reason to be suspicious of you." Bob had a point. As far as Mike White knew, she was just a new soccer ref. "Is that all? Because I really need to get back to football practice. There's a kid playing with a concussion, and I need to stay close."

"Sure. Oh, wait. Do you know if Peter's coach is still mad at him?" She only felt a little guilty for keeping the angel from the injured football player.

Bob frowned. "Not really a pressing issue."

"Do you know or don't you?"

He let out a resigned sigh. "I have no reason to think that Peter's coach is mad at him. In fact, I overheard him praise Peter's aggression to his wife."

"Oh good." She wasn't sure if this was good or not, but she'd take it. "Thanks, Bob." But he was already gone.

She climbed back into the van to see a text message from Nate. "Will you still have time to cook supper?"

Oh good grief. "Yes," she texted back. "I won't let you starve."

Chapter 22

With her family fed and Sammy tucked into bed, Sandra bade farewell to Nate and got ready to step out into the night.

He stopped her at the door and gave her a peck. "Good luck, honey. I still think this is bizarre, but I'm proud of you for it nonetheless."

This admission surprised her and filled her whole body with warmth. Suddenly, she didn't resent pausing the YouTube soccer rules videos to cook him supper. She couldn't remember the last time he'd told her he was proud of her. Had he ever? "Thanks, Nate. See you in a bit." And she stepped out into the crisp autumn air.

Bob was sitting in the passenger seat of her locked minivan. This was simultaneously comforting and creepy. Still, she couldn't help but flash him a smile as she climbed behind the wheel. Her heart pounded with excitement. "Fancy meeting you here."

"What?"

She ignored his lack of a funny bone and started the car. "Too bad I have to drive across town. Can you just grab me and zap us both over there?"

"What?" he said, sounding even more confused than the last time he'd said it.

She turned to look over her shoulder, not entirely trustful of the backup camera. "You know, how you flit around town disappearing and reappearing. Can you make me do that?"

He didn't answer her.

Once she'd backed out onto the street and put the car in drive, she looked at him, but he avoided her gaze. All right then, either he didn't want to admit he couldn't do it, or he wasn't allowed to admit anything. "Is that proprietary information?"

"Do you have a plan?" he asked after an awkward pause.

She snorted. "No, I don't have a plan. Wasn't this your idea? Shouldn't *you* be the one with a plan?"

He stared out the windshield looking contemplative. "Yes, I suppose I should." She didn't know if he was wistfully wishing he had one or actively coming up with one, so she let him think in peace.

Soon, before she was ready, she was pulling into the parking lot of the funeral home on Kirkland Street. As its name suggested, the massive building bore white siding. It also bore far more doors than she thought necessary, and she peered into the darkness, trying to figure out which one to approach. As she stared, she saw a man she didn't recognize striding toward a door near the back. "Maybe we should follow that guy."

"Maybe we should," Bob said and then vanished and reappeared outside the van.

She climbed out and whispered, "Can't you just get out of the vehicle like a normal person?"

"Do you really want someone to see your door opening all by itself?" he whispered back.

Oh yeah, *that*. He had a point. "You ready?" she asked, mostly to stall for herself.

"Waiting on you."

Fine. She willed her legs to move, and found that once she took the first step, the rest followed easily and quickly and soon she was standing inside a well-lit, tastefully appointed hallway. The carpet was so clean that she had the urge to remove her shoes, but before she did so, she realized how weird that would be. Voices drifted down the hall toward her. She couldn't make out what they were saying, but, now in full-sleuth mode, she crept closer, trying to overhear. Bob kept pace with her, staying behind her, and reinforcing her theory that no, if Mike White tried to shove her into a coffin, her angel would *not* be able to stop him. She paused a foot from the doorway and strained to hear.

"We have several policemen working as officials," a man said.

She bit back a gasp. Policemen? That was a good sign, right? She wanted to look at Bob to see if he'd heard, but she didn't dare turn away from the conversation, lest she miss something.

"Well, it's not something I'm dying to do." This new voice was unusually deep. He sounded a little like Robert Barone from *Everybody Loves Raymond*. "I don't even like soccer." He gave a hearty laugh. "But my basketball buddies have guilted me into it."

The original voice laughed. "Whatever it takes. We're desperate for help."

There was a long pause, and Sandra considered giving up the eavesdropping effort.

But then the first voice said, "We'll get started in just a sec. Just waiting on another new ref. The high school principal's wife."

The second voice laughed. "A woman?"

Sandra rolled her eyes.

"Do you have many of those? There's only a few reffing basketball, and I'll tell you, they struggle—"

"Really?" Voice number one, which Sandra had concluded belonged to Mike White, interrupted the Robert Barone wannabee. "Statistics show no such thing. The numbers suggest women make fantastic referees."

Sandra waited nearly a full minute, but Robert had decided to be quiet, and Mike was allowing that to happen, so, with a giant intake of air, she stepped into the open doorway. Instantly, she made eye contact with Mike, who stood to greet her. "Sorry I'm late!" She tried to sound confident and headed for the seat closest to the door, which put her right beside the Robert-impersonator. Mike offered his hand. She shook it, trying to have a firm, manly handshake, and mostly failing.

"You're not late at all. We were early."

She allowed herself to look at Robert. Though he was seated, he was still nearly eye to eye with her. She offered her hand, which he took readily enough. "Hi, I'm Sandra."

"Dwight." Dwight was as tall as Robert, but that's where the similarities ended. Dwight was so pale that Sandra feared he was a vampire. His face was all jagged edges, like it had been chipped out of a cliff.

"Pleasure to meet you, Dwight." She sat down and faced Mike. Faking confidence was making her feel confident. Her heart was still pounding hard enough to hurt, but still, she had this weird inner assurance that she was going to be just fine. She, minivan-driving soccer mom Sandra Provost, could handle this, even if she didn't know quite what this was yet.

Chapter 23

"Thanks for coming," Mike White said in a grave tone. "We're grateful you are here. We are really hurting for refs. I've even had to do some middle school games." His tone made it clear that such an activity was miles beneath him. "And we've even had to cancel a few games."

"Aren't you a college ref?" Robert, scratch that, *Dwight* asked, and Sandra wondered if he would always be such a brown-noser, or if it was a practice he saved for first impressions.

"I am. But when there is a hole and no other official to fill it, either I do it, or we cancel. I don't like to cancel games on middle schoolers." He managed to sound as though he really cared about the children. For a second, Sandra forgot she was looking at someone who might be a murderer.

"Does that mean I'm going to get stuck with all the middle school games?" Dwight asked.

"I would like to volunteer to do solely middle school games," Sandra piped up.

Mike smiled at her. "You'll both be doing middle school this year. Maybe a few JV games if there is no one else to cover, but let's get some experience under your belt before we get too excited. Now, first things first." He slid a rule book across the table to each of them.

Sandra opened hers and squinted down at the tiny print.

"I'm going to assume you know the basics, so I'll just go over recent rule changes with you today."

Sandra wasn't sure this was good news. Just how basic were the basics? If he meant that she needed to know the difference between a corner kick and a goal kick, she might be all right. But if the basics were anything more complicated than that, she might be in trouble.

Mike jumped right in, and he was a fast talker when he wanted to be. Sandra scrambled through her purse for a writing utensil, and panicked when all she could find were two broken crayons and a dried out eyeliner. Mike White read her mind, though, and slid his pen across the table to her. She began to scribble notes, but it was mostly no use. She had a question for nearly every statement he made, and she didn't have the courage to ask them. She knew they were stupid questions, and she didn't want these men to know just how clueless she was.

About fifteen minutes after he started, Mike stopped his instruction and asked if there were any questions. Still, she couldn't think of one that didn't make her sound like a complete moron.

Dwight had a question, of course. "There's a written test, correct?"

Oh man. Of course there would be. She was in trouble. Maybe Bob could help her. That would only be cheating if she really wanted to be a soccer ref, right? She was just doing this to try to solve the Frank Fenton puzzle. Once she'd done that, she would retire back to her normal life. So no, she didn't think it would count as cheating. It would just be part of the undercover process. She fervently hoped Bob would agree to her shaky detective ethics. She could feel him standing behind her and wished she knew what he was thinking. She hoped he was picking up some clues, because she wasn't getting anything. Mike White appeared to be an upstanding professional at the moment.

She realized Mike was talking about the written test and forced herself to focus. "As long as you get it done within a few weeks, you'll be fine."

"And is there a field test?" Dwight asked.

Mike shook his head. "I'll set you up to shadow a mentor ref, pronto. You'll do a game with him or her before you do one on your own." Sandra thought he'd probably added the "for her" for her benefit, and found the gesture to be a kind one.

"Listen to the feedback from that mentor official. I'll put you with ones who know what they're doing. Then, I'll give you a game where you're live, but you'll still be working with that same mentor official. Don't worry, you'll get paid for both games."

It hadn't even occurred to her to wonder about that, but now that he'd mentioned money, the idea cheered her.

"And if the mentor ref thinks you need another shadow game, we can do that too, but that rarely happens. It's a simple game. You guys will be fine."

Right. She'd be fine. What could possibly go wrong?

Mike handed each of them a short stack of paperwork. "Everything else you need to know is right here. Please read through it, and if you have any questions, email me or call me anytime." He looked into her eyes. "I mean it. If you need anything. I want you to be successful, and I'm here for you."

A little freaked out, she dropped his gaze and studied her paperwork. Then, before she was ready, he dismissed their meeting. She panicked. She had not learned a single thing about their case. She searched her brain for a question, any question, she could ask. "You own this funeral home?" Her cheeks grew hot. What a stupid question.

He gave her a broad smile, and there was a twinkle in his eye. Oh great. Not only was it a stupid question, but now he thought she was flirting. "I do, but it's not as weird a profession as you might think."

"I was wondering about that," Dwight said quickly, as if he was jealous that Mike was talking to her instead of him. "How did you ever get involved in this business?"

Mike shrugged. "I'm all about job security," he said and laughed at his own joke. Sandra got the impression it was a joke he'd cracked many times before. She didn't smile, and Dwight laughed as if it was the funniest thing he'd ever heard.

Sandra strained to think of another question, but her mind was blank. She finally allowed herself to look at Bob, hoping he could telepathically communicate an intelligent detective-like question, but he, apparently, was in no mood for telepathy.

"Don't mention Frank. Play it cool," he said right out loud.

She jumped and looked around wildly to see if the men had heard, but they clearly hadn't.

Mike put a hand to the small of her back. "Are you okay?"

Being this close to him, her womanly sixth sense sounded all kinds of alarms. For sure, the guy was a creep. Maybe not a murderer, but definitely a creep. She stepped away from him and nodded. "I'm fine, thanks."

"Okay," he said, sounding skeptical. "You looked like a goose walked over your grave."

"Uh … no… no goose here," she said and then practically ran out of the funeral home.

She jumped into her minivan to find Bob already inside. She held up one hand. "I know, I know, you don't have to say it. I really stink at this. I'm sorry."

His eyes grew wide. "What are you apologizing for? I thought you did great!"

She narrowed her eyes. "You're just saying that because you're an angel, and you have to be nice."

He snorted. "I don't have to be nice. That's not in the angel handbook, and really, you did fine."

She paused, trying to collect herself. "Is there really an angel handbook?"

He laughed. "That's proprietary. And you should really drive away. He's watching."

She hurried to start the van. "Really? Why's he watching?" She stared at the funeral home, but she couldn't see anyone watching. Dwight was still in there, so she thought Mike was probably otherwise engaged. Or maybe they were both watching.

"I don't know why he's watching. I can't read minds. Maybe he's watching because you're sitting in your minivan talking to yourself."

She laughed loudly, and she felt the tight cord of anxiety she'd been living with release with a pleasant snap. "He can't see me. It's dark out."

"I know, but he might wonder why you're still sitting here. You should get home. You've got some studying to do."

She laughed again. "Do I ever. I'm going to be the worst soccer ref in the history of soccer refs."

"Maybe. But by the sounds of it, they probably won't fire you."

Chapter 24

Sandra spent every waking moment trying to learn soccer rules, and she felt she was making great progress. She had it in her mind that she wanted to pass the written test before her shadow game, even though Mike had told her that she had two weeks to do it. Mike had texted her several times "just to check in," and she sensed a vague flirtatious vibe with each message. She answered him as briefly and professionally as possible. "Doing great. Will text you if I have any questions." "Still studying. Will let you know if I need help." But so far, she truly didn't need help. The rules made sense. Most of them followed common sense, and those that didn't, she worked to memorize. She highlighted. She took notes. She quizzed herself. She made Peter quiz her. She tried to make Nate quiz her, but he was too busy. She fell asleep reading the rule book and she watched clips on YouTube while she made dinner.

What she didn't do was go for a run. She had good intentions, but it just never happened. She *thought* about running, planned to run, even bought herself a new pair of (expensive) regulation sneakers, but then they just sat by the door, staying shiny in the box. She didn't have *time* to run. And she didn't want to bother Ethel, not already, not when she would soon be bothering her for every single game. So she focused on the mental preparation, not the physical, not yet. There would be time for that, right?

Then Mike White called—three days after her first and only training meeting, during which precious little training had taken place. "Can you do a shadow game tomorrow at nine?"

"What?" She was certain she'd misheard him.

"I'm pairing you with Birch Kabouya."

"I'm sorry, could you repeat that?" He hadn't said *Birch*, had he, as in a *birch* tree? And why was she suddenly craving kombucha?

"Birch Ka-*boo*-ya," he said, over-enunciating this time. "He's good people, one of my best, and he's looking forward to helping you. He doesn't want to do any more middle school games either." Mike paused to laugh. "So he's happy to have fresh meat."

A wave of nausea washed over her. She didn't like being called meat, no matter what the context.

"So, can you make it?"

She scanned her schedule. Yes, she thought she could. Oh wait, it was ladies' craft day at church. She had already paid for the supplies. But she could miss it, couldn't she? Sure. They probably wouldn't even notice she was gone. "Sure. Where?"

"Fryeburg Middle School."

Fryeburg? That was a kazillion miles away. "Seriously?"

"Don't worry. I'll make sure you get paid mileage."

"Okay." She didn't know what else to say.

"Great. Did you get your uniform yet?"

Of course not. She'd only ordered it three days ago. "Nope."

"No problem. Just wear something comfortable, and have fun."

Her heart did a weird little leap at the word "fun." This had the potential for fun? That hadn't occurred to her yet. Several other thoughts had: *When is Nate going to talk to Ethan's and Jack's parents? Did Mike White kill Frank, and how am I going to figure that out? Is Frank innocent, and if so, how can I clear his name? I need to learn the soccer rules. I need to study the soccer rules. How am I going to learn all these stupid soccer rules?*

But she hadn't thought about having fun. In fact, *fun* was a fairly foreign concept at this stage of her life. Sure, she had things she enjoyed: Sammy falling asleep and allowing her to watch an episode of *Downton Abbey* uninterrupted. Or ordering a pizza so she didn't have to cook supper. Or eating chocolate chips straight out of the bag. But she wasn't sure these things counted as *fun.* She'd stopped having fun years ago, hadn't she? So the idea that fun was about to reenter her life sent an almost-guilty thrill coursing through her veins. Fun? Sure, why not? Let's give it a shot! "Okay, I will. Thanks."

"You bet. And check your online schedule. I've already assigned you some games." Before she could express her disbelief at this announcement, he said goodbye and hung up. She hurried toward her laptop but then couldn't find it. Where was it? She flung things around in a mad search and found it underneath a pile of unfolded laundry. She collapsed into said pile, flipped the computer open, and then waited impatiently as the system logged her in. And then there it was. Her first game. Monday afternoon. She swallowed hard. Suddenly, fun seemed unlikely

.

Chapter 25

Sandra drove to Fryeburg with a heavy blanket of guilt wrapped snug around her shoulders. Nate had made it clear that he was not happy to be stuck with three children all day. He'd called it "babysitting," as though they weren't his kids. She tried to shake it off, tried to remind herself that Nate had given her his blessing for this whole thing, had even told her he was proud of her. Maybe he was just cranky. He had a lot on his mind.

She turned her discontent toward her angel. Where was Bob, anyway? A horrific thought dawned. What if Fryeburg was outside his zone? No! It couldn't be! No way could she do this without him! Before she realized it was happening, her fear morphed into anger. How dare he leave her out here dangling like this? This was *his* idea! Now she had to go meet someone named Birch, run for the first time since her failed attempt at high school softball, and try to solve a crime all by herself? She was so furious that her eyes blurred with tears. This made her even angrier. It didn't matter the emotion—hers all manifested in tears: sadness, fear, anger, even joy. Always crying. She swatted at her cheeks and then she saw him. At least she thought it was him.

Up ahead stood a short, stocky man with his thumb out in the air. If it wasn't Bob, it certainly looked like him. But she didn't dare pick him up, did she? What if it wasn't him? She slowed down to get a better look, and he gave her a wide smile. It *was* him. What on earth was he doing?

She slammed on the brakes, and he trotted over to the car. "Can I git a ride?" he asked, trying for a local accent—and failing.

"What are you doing?"

Without permission, he opened the door and got in.

"Wait, are you visible right now?"

"Yep. Didn't want people to wonder why you were pulling over. But I'll turn it off in a sec." He looked out the windshield. "Let's go."

"Why are you hitchhiking?" she cried.

He motioned toward the road, as if to say he wasn't going to answer her until she drove. When she pulled back out into traffic, he said, "I was trying to make a *Highway to Heaven* joke, but I guess you're not familiar with the show."

She scowled, wondering whether she should smack him or not. "I am *quite* familiar with the show," she said, sounding overly defensive but unable to reel it in, "but your joke still doesn't make any sense."

Bob's eyes grew wide. "You know, in the beginning. Jonathan is walking down the road, and Victor picks him up."

"But he wasn't hitchhiking!" Sandra cried. "Victor just recognized him and pulled over!"

Bob looked thoughtful. "Oh yeah, you might be right. Anyway, about this game. Are you ready?"

But she wasn't ready for the conversation to transition. "What if someone else had pulled over?"

"Well, then, I would've asked *them* for a ride to Fryeburg."

She doubted that. She also didn't know what else to say. So she gave up. "No, I am most certainly not ready for this. I am fully expecting to keel over and die right there in the grass."

He looked at her, surprised. "What do you mean?"

She shook her head. "Never mind." She'd keep her physical fitness, or lack thereof, to herself for the time being. It would become public knowledge soon enough. She turned on her blinker and slowed to take the turn, but Bob protested.

"Where are you going?"

She glanced down at the GPS. "To the Fryeburg Middle School."

He put his hand on the dashboard, as if that would stop her from making the turn. She wondered if he *did* have the power to stop her car from turning. "This is not the right road."

"It is so! Look at the map!"

"I am an angel of the Lord! I am smarter than your map app!"

His incidental rhyme would have been funny, but the tone of his voice obliterated any inkling of humor. That was the first time she'd ever heard him raise his voice, and it was an intimidating sound, despite his less than intimidating image. She turned her blinker off and returned her foot to the accelerator. "Sorry."

"No, *I'm* sorry. I get a bit defensive on occasion."

She bit back a grin. "Fair enough. So do I."

After a tense minute of carpooling, Bob said, "Take the next left."

She did as she was told, and after a short, bumpy ride, a soccer field rose into view. "You were right."

He didn't say anything.

She pulled into a parking spot. "Are you staying here for the whole game?"

He nodded. "I plan to. Unless there's a crisis."

She took a deep, shaky breath. "I hope there isn't one. I take great comfort in the fact that you're here."

He put a gentle hand on her forearm. She looked down at it and saw that she was still white-knuckling the steering wheel. She willed herself to relax.

"You're going to be great. Trust me. I've watched a lot of soccer games. I know things."

For reasons she couldn't identify, she believed him, and her nerves nearly abated. "Should we have a code word or something?"

He snickered. "What? What do you mean?"

"I mean, if I need you, I can't exactly call out, 'Angel Bob! Come quick!' now, can I?"

He gave her a sideways smile. "You can if you want. Or, you can just say a silent prayer, and then God will give me my orders."

Her mouth dropped open. "Does God send angels every time someone asks?"

At first he said nothing, so she said, "Proprietary?" realizing halfway through the word that he was saying the same word himself. She laughed. "Jinx." She pulled her baseball cap on, partly to shield her eyes from the sun and partly to hide her face, and then she stepped out of her minivan.

Chapter 26

As Sandra made her way to the field, she could no longer see Bob, but she could still feel his presence. She didn't know how close he was, but she knew he was there.

A tall, lanky man wearing a fluorescent yellow shirt came running toward her with his hand extended. His long dreadlocks were gathered into a ponytail on the top of his head, the ends of them springing out in all directions, making him look like a failed prototype of a Trolls doll.

She did not need an introduction, but he gave one anyway. "Birch Kabouya at your service!" he announced with an exuberance she thought excessive.

With trepidation, she took his offered hand into her own and then tried not to grimace at its dampness. She couldn't blame the man. His flushed cheeks and glistening forehead suggested he'd already been running around. But it was still gross. The realization that she'd soon be just as sweaty and gross, if not sweatier and grosser, was cold comfort.

"I'm so, so excited that you've decided to do this, man. All us refs are! Do you have any friends who want to ref too? Do you have any questions for me yet?" If she had any, he gave her no chance to voice them. "As we get going, feel free to ask me things. I might not be able to answer you right away, as this is a real game that counts and everything, we usually start new refs with preseason games that don't count, but that's okay, we're still glad you're here, so even if I'm not looking at you, I can still hear you, so go right ahead and ask, and I'll answer when I get a chance, okay?" This was the chattiest man she'd ever encountered. Was he *on* something? "So, before the game, you need to check the field, do a perimeter walk or jog, and check the nets and everything. You know."

She didn't know. Check the nets for what?

"And the posts. Don't forget the posts."

Right. She didn't know what he wanted her to do about the posts, but she wouldn't forget them.

"I've already done the perimeter, and pretty soon we're going to do the coin flip. Do you have a coin yet?"

Yes. She owned a coin, but she kept mum about it. All her loose change was back in her van's cup holder, covered in embarrassing crusty coffee and fuzz. Besides, she needed to conserve her energy.

He reached into his chest pocket and pulled out a giant fake coin. "You can just use a regular coin if you want, but eventually, you'll want to get one of these. They're only like six bucks, and they're easier to see."

She could not imagine spending six bucks on a fake coin.

"Oh look! There's the other ref. I've worked with him before. He's good people. Come on"—he started to walk away—"I'll introduce you."

Sandra hurried to keep up with Birch, and was somewhat relieved to observe that the second ref appeared to be far less energetic. He waited for them to reach him before extending his hand. "Bob Bernier."

Uh-oh. It was going to be confusing to have two Bobs around.

"People call me Moose."

Good. One problem solved.

She shook his hand. "Sandra Provost. Pleasure to meet you."

Moose looked at Birch. "So that explains it. I wondered why you had a middle school game. I haven't reffed with you in years, since back when you were just starting out."

Birch laughed as though that was the funniest thing he'd ever heard. "I've done lots of 'em this year. This year's been hard. Not enough of us to go around, so White keeps asking me to do these junior high games. But I don't mind. It's like a vacation. The game is so much slower, I barely have to run."

The expression on Moose's face made it clear that this last comment annoyed him. Clear to her, at least. Maybe not to Birch, who was still talking about how many games he'd reffed. Listening to him, she understood why people were so excited she'd signed up for the gig. Birch had games every day except for Sunday, and on many days, he did two games. She couldn't imagine running up and down the field for one entire game, let alone two. How was she going to do this? What had she been thinking? Birch joked about all the money he was raking in, then complained about two schools who still owed him hundreds of dollars each, and then finished up his monologue by detailing how much physical therapy he was doing on his knees. She glanced at them, but they looked like normal—albeit knobby—knees.

Moose smiled at her, as if amused that she was staring at Birch's jumbo patellae. "You're shadowing one of the best. This guy can be a pain in the rump, but he's a good official. You got lucky. White's got that other new guy, the cop who is pale as a ghost, shadowing Dodge."

"Jeepers!" Birch cried. Then he looked at her and sort of whispered, "Dodge is a drunk."

She nodded because she didn't know what else to do. It was hard to feel sorry for Dwight.

"Right," Moose said, "but they're both basketball refs, so birds of a feather and all that. Let's get this thing done. I've got a pot roast and a pie to get home to."

The mention of food made Sandra's nervous tummy tumble. Wasn't it a bit early in the day for pot roast? Birch followed him to midfield, and Sandra, left without instruction, wondered if she was supposed to follow as well. When they reached the intersection of midfield and the sideline, Birch noticed she wasn't alongside him and waved at her impatiently. She swallowed her annoyance. If he'd told her to follow, she would've followed. Was she supposed to read his mind? She trotted over to where the two officials and team captains were now standing in a small circle. Birch enthusiastically introduced himself, and then Moose followed suit, calling himself "Bob" not "Moose" and using less enthusiasm than his counterpart had. Sandra did not introduce herself, though the young athletes still shook her hand as if she mattered. She wondered what they thought of her, standing there in her almost-too-tight workout clothes that looked brand-new. She'd only taken the tags off them today, but she'd bought them a long time ago, one day when they'd been on sale and she'd been high on good intentions.

The home team won the toss and chose to have the ball. The purple team—Sandra had already forgotten who they were, and their jerseys only said Tigers—chose their goal. Birch turned and ran across the field, and this time she followed, barely getting to the other side before he blew his whistle and the game began. Wait! The game had already started? She wasn't ready! She didn't even know what she was supposed to be doing! The ball was already six feet from the goal, and she was still frozen in place. This was madness! She would never catch up. *Here we go*, she told herself in a voice that sounded vaguely like herself, but unlike anything she'd heard in years. *You're going to do this if it kills you. But it won't kill you.*

Sandra put her head down and ran.

Chapter 27

Sandra thought she might be having a heart attack. She couldn't catch her breath and was embarrassed by how her chest was heaving up and down. Her calves were on fire, and she stretched them every time the action stopped, but it made no difference. Perhaps the most difficult portion of the ordeal, however, was the inadequacy of her sports bra. It just wasn't doing its job, and she was enduring the pain that proved it. She had never been so excited to go bra shopping. In fact, she wasn't going home until she had the best sports bra money could buy. Maybe they made one out of metal. Maybe they could weld one onto her, a custom fit. Anything but this. She considered running with one arm across her chest, but the potential embarrassment trumped the pain, and she suffered through it.

Through all this, she tried to pay attention to the game. She really did. She tried to watch for fouls, tried to understand why Birch blew his whistle, and tried to pay attention to his hand signals—but all she could think about was surviving the next step. She ran and ran. Up and down. She'd sprint with all her might in order to reach the eighteen just as some giant eighth grader pounded it back to his striker. And she would turn and sprint again, her inner chest burning and her outer chest aching. And when the buzzer signaled the end of the first half, she almost fell to her knees and wept with relief.

Unfortunately, neither Moose nor Birch collapsed into the grass, so it felt a little too conspicuous to do so. So, hands on her hips, and breathing so deeply her chest made a rasping sound, she strode across the field, to where Birch was already conferring with Moose. To her dismay, she saw there were only five minutes on the clock. Five minutes? A five-minute half-time? That was no half-time at all! She fondly recalled those days when she'd only been a soccer mom, those days when half-time had seemed to stretch on forever, those days that were only yesterday. How she missed those days.

She decided then that this had been a fool's errand. They would have to find a different way to infiltrate the officials' inner circle. She wasn't even ashamed. She'd tried. She'd given it her best shot. She reached the referees and opened her mouth to resign, but Moose cut her off.

"Go get your trainee a bottle of water." It came out like an order, giving Birch no opportunity to decline, and he ran off toward the snack shack.

Moose put a hand on her shoulder, and she was embarrassed, realizing how sweaty that shoulder must be. He didn't seem to notice, though. "Sandra, right?"

She nodded. She couldn't speak.

"Sandra, you are running too much."

Surprised, she tried to laugh, but she sounded like a bloodhound with laryngitis.

"If you spend that much time running, you can't see any of the game. You rarely have to go all the way to the goal line, and you definitely don't have to go to the goal line on my end of the field. You can stop at the eighteen down there."

She stared up into his eyes, trying to convey her confusion. She didn't understand. She wasn't even running as much as Birch was running.

"I know, I know. Birch is an idiot and runs too much." He'd read her mind. "He's running even more today than usual. I think he's just trying to impress you. Or maybe he's got so much nervous energy that he can't help it. But anyone who runs that much is going to miss stuff. Trust me. I've been doing this for a hundred years."

A hundred years. There. There was her opening. She had to say something. But could she speak? She glanced toward the snack shack, and Birch was already on his way back. She opened her mouth to try. "A hundred years?" she managed. Now she sounded like an old lady who'd just inhaled helium, but at least the bloodhound was gone. For now. "So you must have known Frank?" With each word, she started to sound more like a normal person.

Moose's face fell. "Of course. We've reffed together for years. He was the best." Moose chuckled. "I kept telling him to retire, and he'd always tell me he'd die on the field. Guess he knew what he was doing."

"But someone killed him," Sandra said quickly, knowing she was out of time.

Moose studied her face as Birch appeared beside her, handing her a water bottle.

"Thanks." She told her arm to move to grab the bottle, and it sluggishly obeyed. Then, she was almost too weak to unscrew the cap.

"Who killed someone?" Birch asked.

Moose shook his head slowly, and Sandra regretted upsetting him. She was terrible at this. Why had she spoken so crassly? Usually, she had more class than that.

"We were just talking about ole Frank." Moose reached out and grabbed the only remaining water bottle from Birch's hand, unscrewed the cap, and chugged half the bottle.

Though Sandra was certain that Birch had meant that water for himself, as he hadn't made any indication of handing it off to his partner, he didn't even seem to notice the bottle was missing from his hand. He just stared at Sandra awkwardly. "What about him?"

Whoa. Birch looked guilty. She searched her brain for words. The buzzer sounded. She was out of time, and she hadn't even resigned yet. "I was just saying how weird it is that he was murdered in the middle of a soccer game."

With the goofy smile wiped off his face, several deep wrinkles made Birch look much older than she'd originally thought he was. "I have a hard time believing he was even murdered." He glanced at Moose and gave a cheesy fake laugh. "I mean, who would kill Frank?"

Moose polished off the water and tossed the bottle toward a duffel bag on the sideline, where another empty bottle already lay. "I don't know, but I hope they catch the guy and string him up." Then Moose headed across the field, to the side Sandra and Birch had trod during the first half. Sandra assumed then that officials switched sides after halftime. Or maybe Moose just wanted a change of scenery.

Birch gave her one more long, cryptic look and then blew the whistle. A tiny child with orange hair kicked the ball, and the clock started again. Birch took off like his pants were on fire. Sandra quickly drank half the water in her bottle and then threw it toward the duffel bag that was apparently collecting them. Then she turned toward Birch and gave chase. But she did a lot less running in the second half, and after only a few minutes, decided that

Moose was her new favorite person in the world.

Chapter 28

Sandra's legs felt as though they'd been put through the wringer. Twice. Yet, as she lay awake beside her snoring husband, she felt an odd euphoria. While she hadn't actually reffed a soccer game, she *had* survived one, and she couldn't remember the last time she'd felt so good about herself.

Nowhere near sleep, she wasn't sure which was keeping her awake: the incessant pain in her legs or the nagging feeling that she'd found a clue during that soccer game and didn't know what it was. On the way home, Bob the angel had asked her what she'd learned, and she'd said, "Moose is an innocent gem of a man, and Birch is likable but suspicious." But wasn't there more than that? Hadn't she seen, heard, or smelled something else? Like a word on the tip of her tongue, she knew it was there, but she couldn't quite spit it out. Unlike a word on the tip of her tongue, she feared she really needed this clue. She couldn't just use another word. She was truly missing something.

She went over the details of her day, trying to summon up something relevant, but couldn't force her way into an epiphany. She prayed about it, but there was no return mail via the supernatural express. Maybe she should *stop* thinking about it. Then maybe it would come to her? She dug through the stack of books on the bottom shelf of her nightstand until she found her e-reader. She hadn't opened the thing in months, but if she turned on a light to read, Nate was sure to wake up and be irritated. So she flipped open the small technological miracle in her hands and flipped through the books she'd downloaded over the few years she'd owned the device. Nothing really excited her, and she was beginning to think the e-reader had been a bad idea when a new thought excited her.

Mystery novels! Wasn't she acting just like one of those amateur sleuths in those novels? She was like Harry without the Corgi. Or Sookie without the vampires. She hadn't read a mystery in years, but it was now high time. Surely reading about other small-town sleuths would help. Or maybe she should read the soccer rule book. Nah, that wasn't available in ebook. Mystery for the win!

She browsed the bookstore until she found one that looked intriguing and then hit download. *That's the way to shop*, she thought. *Especially when my legs are broken.*

She read herself to sleep, dropping the e-reader beside her pillow as the dreams took over. She dreamed she was reffing a soccer game where all the players seemed too tiny to be in middle school. In the dream, she agonized over whether to make sure the kids were old enough to play. Should she ask the coach? How embarrassed she'd be if, of course, they were certainly old enough, but they were just small, and she'd just insulted the whole lot of them. Deep under layers of blankets and sleep, she hemmed and hawed. Ask the coach or start the game? Finally, she decided she had to ask the coach, but when she turned to do so, the coach had turned into a giant panda bear.

It sat there looking at her, chomping on some bamboo. She turned to look at the other coach, almost certain that she too, had become a panda.

She had. Both coaches were pandas. And then all the players were pandas too, only they were no longer tiny. They were giant pandas, all over the field, and she could no longer see the ball because it blended in so well with all the pandas.

She sat bolt upright in bed, her movement so sudden that a long stab of pain reached down her back and into her legs. "Ow!" she cried out, but whether from the pain or the sudden fear of giant pandas, she didn't know.

"What is it?" Nate asked. He reached over and started to rub her back. "Bad dream?"

She lay back down and tried to catch her breath. Now that reality was coming into focus, the dream became more ridiculous and less scary, and she began to giggle—a nervous giggle that still quivered with fear. "Yeah, just a stupid dream. Sorry I woke you up."

"No problemo," he said, and she could tell from the thickness of his voice that he was already falling back asleep.

Pandas. Of all the weirdness she'd encountered in the last few days, that might take the cake. She picked up her sleeping e-reader and went back into her mystery. Her legs still hurt, and her euphoria remained. In no hurry for morning, she found herself immensely enjoying the company her new book gave her as the minutes ticked by.

Chapter 29

Nate's alarm jerked her out of a deep panda-free sleep. She opened one eye to peer at the clock. Seven o'clock. The latest she'd slept in ages.

Nate pounded the snooze button, rolled over, and pulled the covers over his head.

Without the blaring alarm, the house was far too quiet. Why couldn't she hear Sammy? Trying not to panic, she tried to leap out of bed to check on him, but her body wouldn't cooperate. Her muscles had turned to hard, unyielding sticks of lumber, and when her feet hit the floor, they screamed in protest. As she stood up straight, her lower back let out a crack that sounded like a nearby clap of thunder. It felt glorious. Encouraged by that odd feeling of release, she dragged her bare feet toward Sammy's room.

His crib was empty. Her heart started to thump. Had Mike White stolen her baby?! *Sorry, God. It was stupid to think I was some sort of sleuth. I'll stop, I promise. Just help me find Sammy.* When she stepped back out into the hallway, she heard the television. That was weird. Joanna must be up.

But it wasn't Joanna. As the couch came into view, she saw the back of Peter's head.

"Peter!" she cried and then winced at the panic in her voice. "Do you know where Sammy is?"

Oblivious to her panic, he mumbled, "Yeah, he's right here."

She came around the corner of the couch to see Sammy perched in Peter's lap, chewing on his thumb, and staring at the Minecraft video playing on YouTube. Air rushed out of Sandra's lungs as she collapsed onto the couch beside them. Instinct told her to yank her youngest from Peter's arms, but she stopped herself. This was unusual behavior on Peter's part, but she wanted to encourage it. "Why do you have him?"

At first, Peter ignored her. He was so engrossed in whatever was happening on the screen.

She gently elbowed him.

"What? Oh. He was crying, and I figured you needed your sleep after your big game." He smirked at her, and she didn't know if he was making fun of her.

"Well, thank you. I *did* need some sleep, and I didn't get much last night. You got him for another minute? I need coffee."

"Sure. Until he cries or poops, we're good."

She laughed and tousled Peter's hair, her heart swelling with pride and affection. He was such a great young man, and she would think that even if he wasn't her kid.

Her brain told her body to stand up, and nothing happened. Oh no. She was stuck on the couch. She leaned back. There were worse things. Maybe she could just stay home today and recuperate. But first, she needed coffee, and she didn't trust Peter to make it correctly. She tried again, pushing back into the couch cushions this time to try to gain some rebound power.

She almost made it, but then fell back into the worn leather.

Maybe it was time to quit coffee. Or maybe she should hail an angel and have him supernaturally heave her off the sofa.

Peter looked at her. "Are you okay?"

She laughed. "I'm not sure. I think I'm too old for soccer." An image of Frank appeared in her head, and she realized the absurdity of what she'd just said. Not too old. Just too out of shape.

She needed a different plan. She allowed herself to topple over sideways so that the top half of her was horizontal. This position felt lovely, so she lingered there for a bit. Then she twisted her upper half so her hands were under her, and did a push-up as she dragged her feet under her.

Oh good. This was working. Almost there. With a grunt, she pushed herself to her feet and then slowly straightened up. Disappointingly, her back did not crack this time.

"That was graceful."

Sammy made a gurgling sound that sounded like agreement.

"Zip it, both of you." Feeling accomplished, she headed for the coffee pot. When she reached the counter, she heard her husband stirring and was glad she'd made it off the couch before he too had witnessed the struggle.

Chapter 30

Sandra left adult Sunday school under the pretense of using a restroom. She didn't actually announce this, of course, but she knew that's what everyone assumed she was doing. Why else would she leave in the middle of class? Well, to snoop around and make sure no one was picking on her son—that's why.

Trying to be invisible, she peeked through the small window in Peter's classroom door. Unfortunately, Peter sat facing the window, and she jerked her face out of his view. Though her body had loosened up immensely, this sudden change of motion caused muscles she didn't even know she had to cry out in protest.

Deep breath. He hadn't seen her. But she hadn't seen *anything*.

She couldn't resist the temptation of a second look. She slid one eye toward the glass and immediately made eye contact with her son. She jerked her face away from the pane again. This was silly. She still hadn't seen anything. And there was no need to be sneaky, now that she'd been caught, as Peter appeared to be the only one facing the window. So she just blatantly looked inside.

It was evident that her son was furious with her. She didn't care. He sat alone on one side of the table, with his tablet in front of him. Two girls sat on an adjacent side, pressed so closely together they seemed to be wearing the same outfit. And there were Jack and Ethan, on the opposite side of the table. The scene looked amicable enough, but Sandra's stomach was unsettled. Something was amiss, whether she could see it or not.

She heard a familiar noise, but by the time she placed it, it was too late. The door swung open, and the bottom ridge of the window smashed her in the face. She cried out, more in surprise than in pain, though it had certainly hurt, and staggered backward. The teacher appeared in the doorway. Where had *she* been lurking? And why was Jack's mother teaching Peter's Sunday school class?

"Oh, I'm so sorry!" Casey said, sounding sincere enough.

"Tis okay," Sandra said through her nose, sounding like she'd suddenly come down with a terrible head cold.

Casey motioned toward the open doorway, as if Sandra had been trying to come inside, maybe even preparing to knock like a normal, polite person would, before the collision had occurred.

"No, thank you," Sandra said, pulling her hand away from her face, hoping that would take away some of the new overpowering nasal quality. "I just needed to talk to Peter."

He looked surprised, but unbothered by this news. He grabbed his tablet and was standing beside her outside of the classroom in less than a second. She smiled at him and turned to walk away. As expected, he followed. She opened the door to the stairwell, and they both stepped inside.

As soon as the door clicked shut behind them, Peter whispered, "What are you doing?"

"I was just checking on you!"

"I don't need checking on. I'm not a baby!"

"I know that, honey. Why is Jack's mother teaching your class?"

Peter shrugged. "Mr. Emmons is sick, I guess. It's okay, though. Jack is better when she's around."

"So they're not giving you any trouble today?"

Peter looked at the carpet.

This was ridiculous. She wasn't sending him back in there. "You want to go get a coffee?"

He wrinkled up his nose. "Not really."

She knew he thought she meant a weak coffee from the dirty coffee pot in the church kitchen, and he didn't even drink coffee. She snickered. "No, I mean a real coffee from Dunkin', and I meant that *I* would be the one drinking it."

He smiled. "Can I get a donut?"

"If you don't tell your sister. I've got to go grab my purse. Meet you in the car."

He vanished up the stairs, taking three of them at a time.

She didn't really want to return to Sunday school to retrieve her purse and then disappear again, but she thought the price was worth the gain of spending time with Peter and keeping him away from Jack and Ethan. Besides, she could get a donut too. She'd earned one, after all the calories she'd burned the day before, right?

Chapter 31

"What did Ethan's parents say?" Sandra asked Nate as soon as they were alone in their living room.

Nate sighed as if he was sick of talking about it, though they hadn't talked about it yet. He slowly pulled off his church shoes, and Sandra struggled to be patient. "Roger said he'd take care of it."

Something about his tone made her suspicious. But she knew that Nate never lied to her. Was her new sleuthing hobby making her less trusting? Or maybe more attune to sniffing out liars? She didn't know how to proceed. He was done talking about it. She wasn't. And she didn't believe what he'd just told her.

After a long pause, she said, "And?"

He pulled his eyes away from the football game on the screen. "And what?"

"And what else did he say?"

Nate stared at her as if sizing her up. Then he rubbed at his jaw as he returned his eyes to the television. "I really don't think there's anything to worry about, Sandy. At first, he just laughed it off and said that kids squabble, but I told him that wasn't good enough, and then he said he'd have a talk with Ethan." He paused. "And I don't see what else we can do. That will have to be good enough."

That was *so* not good enough. Sandra wasn't one for drama, especially church drama, but this situation called for some pot stirring. "And did you talk to Jack's parents?"

"Didn't see them."

What a crock. She'd known for a fact that Jack's mom had been there. She tried to stand up abruptly, using her body language to communicate that she was done doing things Nate's way, but her body moved too slowly to communicate anything. Just sitting on the couch had stiffened everything up again. When she headed for the door instead of the kitchen, Nate asked, "Where are you going?"

"Going to invite Casey to coffee." *And I'm going to see just how much coffee a woman can consume in a day.*

"Honey, don't do that. What about lunch?"

She held back the groan that was trying to launch. "There are cold cuts in the fridge." She grabbed her purse and left, taking care not to slam the door behind her. As she walked down the front steps, she looked through her contacts for Casey's numbers, but of course, she didn't have it. She didn't want to go back inside for the church directory. But she couldn't just show up at the woman's door, could she? That would be rude.

Yes, she could just show up at the woman's door. Desperate times, desperate measures.

She had to drive around a couple of blocks to remember where Casey even lived. She'd been there for a ladies' tea, but that had been years ago, and they'd painted the house since then. She was thankful to recognize Casey's SUV, and she pulled in behind it. Then she took her time walking to the door, in part to give them time to see her through the window, and in part because every step felt like dying. When she was done with this, she was going to go home and watch *Murder, She Wrote* for the rest of the day. She couldn't wait for tomorrow. She would feel so much better tomorrow. Good thing too, as she had her first game. Shoot. Maybe she should be studying the rule book right now instead of out picking fights with church moms. Casey opened her front door. Too late now.

"Hi, Sandra! What can I do for you?" Casey was still in her church clothes. For reasons Sandra couldn't identify, this annoyed her.

"Hi, Casey. I was wondering if I could buy you a cup of coffee."

Casey tipped her head to the side and studied her for several seconds. Then she stepped to the side. "I'm not sure I have the energy to go out, but you're welcome to come in."

Sandra didn't want to go in. She wanted to have this conversation on neutral turf. But she wasn't sure how to make that happen. So, grudgingly, she stepped inside. Immediately, she was annoyed at how immaculate the place was. Did anyone even live here?

Casey swept her arm toward her living room, where her husband Lewis sat, also still in his church clothes. It sure appeared as though he had been there too. "Please, have a seat," Casey said.

Sandra knew then that she had already been beaten. This wasn't going to change anything. It might even make things worse. Should she change her mind, apologize? Say she made a mistake? Would that be a better course than the one she was about to endure? Or worse?

Casey decided for her. "So, you're here to talk about how the boys are getting along?"

Chapter 32

Sandra sat down, trying to hide how much this hurt. Lewis gave her a fake smile, and Casey perched on the armrest beside him. Sandra wished she were anywhere else. She wished she were chasing Birch up and down a soccer field.

"Yes. I don't mean to be overly protective, but I just want the boys to get along. Church should be a safe place for children—"

"Church *is* a safe place for children," Lewis cut her off with a stern voice that confirmed what she already knew. This battle was lost.

She tried to smile. "Maybe we could get the boys together and talk it—"

It was Casey's turn to interrupt. "We've already talked to Jack, and he has promised that he will work harder at getting along with Peter."

Getting along with? That wasn't the phrase she would have used. Maybe, "work harder at not bullying Peter" would be better. "That would be great," she said. "Thanks for your time." She stood to go.

"Just so you know, the boys say that Peter doesn't work very hard at fitting in."

She turned to look at Casey. What? What on earth did that mean? "I'm sorry?"

Casey stood. "Nothing to be sorry for." Sandra was certain she'd never heard a more patronizing tone. "I just wanted you to know that Jack and Ethan are not entirely to blame here. Peter also needs to make an effort to get along better with his peers."

Sandra forced a smile that she feared looked too much like a vampire about to lunge. "Of course. I'll talk to him." She turned and nearly ran for the door, opened it and let herself out before Casey could do it.

She managed to hold back the tears until she got into the minivan, but then they came. She could not believe how cold those two people had just been to her. Nate had been right. She should drop it. She would tell Peter to ignore them. Everyone had to deal with bullies, right? She still felt people shouldn't have to deal with them at church, but maybe God was toughening Peter up for something.

Relief washed over her as she pulled back into her own driveway. Ignoring her husband, who was engrossed in the football game, she microwaved herself a bag of popcorn, discreetly dumped in a couple handfuls of chocolate chips, and then checked on Sammy, who was sound asleep in his crib. Grateful for that small gift, she secreted herself in her bedroom. She'd fought against Nate when he'd wanted to put a TV in the bedroom, but now she was grateful. She turned on Netflix and climbed onto the blessedly soft bed. She found *Murder, She Wrote* and pressed play.

A soft knock sounded on her door. She groaned and pressed pause. Her mini-vacation was already over. "Come in," she called, trying to sound loving.

The door opened slowly to reveal Peter. She tried to hide her surprise. She'd been expecting Joanna. "Hi, honey. What's up?"

He gingerly sat down on the foot of her bed. "I heard you and Dad talking."

Shoot. "Okay." She didn't know what else to say.

"I told you it wouldn't do any good."

She decided to level with him. "And you were right."

He blinked, surprised. Then he smiled. "So I take it coffee didn't go well either?"

"She didn't want coffee, and no, it didn't go well. I'm sorry that you're going through this, honey. I don't think the parents are going to be much help. I can go to church leadership if you want?" She expected him to adamantly object, but he didn't.

He appeared to be thinking it over. "Maybe."

"Maybe?"

He studied the wall for several seconds. "I'll let you know." He stood to go. Then he looked at her. "Thanks for trying, Mom. I didn't really want you to, but I know why you did it." He gave her a smile that looked sort of sad.

"I sure do love you, honey. I'm sorry growing up is so hard."

"I know you do. And growing up isn't so bad, most of the time." He left her room, gently closing the door behind him. She was glad the boy had soccer, glad he was good at something, glad he had another place to be safe and have friends.

She settled back into the pillows and restarted her TV show, though she'd lost interest in both it and her chocolaty popcorn.

The Whistle Blower

Chapter 33

Considering how many troubles Sandra was currently juggling in her life, she woke up in a slamming good mood on Monday morning. That is, until she sat up.

Against all expectations, her lameness had not dissipated during the night. In fact, it had intensified. She sat there on the edge of her bed wrestling with reality. How was this possible? She'd had lame muscles on several occasions over the years, and they had never lasted more than twenty-four hours. Was something wrong? Had she injured herself? Should she seek medical attention?

Nate stepped into the room, fresh out of the shower. She paused her worry to enjoy the fresh smell of him, but her worry bounced right back to the surface. "Honey, I'm even sorer than I was yesterday. How is that possible?"

Without looking at her, he laughed heartily. "You're getting old."

"What?" She was so not getting old. She wasn't even forty yet, for crying out loud.

"It's true, trust me. It's happened to me too. The older we get, the longer it takes our muscles to recover."

She cried out in anguish and flopped back down on the bed. "No! That's terrible news! I have another game today."

"I didn't tell you to be a soccer ref."

Nope, he hadn't. But did that mean she wasn't allowed to talk about it? She squeezed her eyes shut.

He gently sat down beside her. "Where does it hurt?" he asked softly.

She moaned. "Everywhere."

He chuckled. "Everywhere? Are you sure?"

She nodded without opening her eyes. "I'm sure. My hair follicles hurt."

He ran a hand through her hair, which felt lovely. "Once you get running and warm your muscles up, you'll be fine." He kissed her on the forehead. "I've got to get ready and head out, but I just wanted to tell you that I'm proud of you. I still think this whole thing is a little nuts, but I'm proud of you."

She smiled up at him. "Thanks, Nate." She watched him finish getting dressed and leave the room, and then she peeled herself from the bed and headed toward the kitchen and the coffee pot. She was beyond grateful that he'd already brewed a pot, and she poured herself a generous serving, which she carried with her as she hobbled down the hallway to wake her kids up.

Another week was about to begin, whether they wanted it to or not.

With two kids deposited, she returned home determined to study her soccer rule book and take her test. But Bob was waiting on her porch swing.

"I've missed you," she said as she approached.

"You have?" He looked so hopeful that she snickered.

"Sure. Get used to having an angel around, and you miss him when he's gone." She unlocked her front door, and he came to stand beside her, taking for granted that she wanted him to follow her inside.

He was right. She was thrilled for the company.

As soon as they were safely inside, he asked, "What's the plan for today?"

She snickered. "The plan is to try to live through another soccer game, only, I guess, this time Birch will be shadowing me, instead of the other way around."

"I meant, what are we going to do about our murder investigation?"

She laughed at him. She couldn't help it. Was he pretending that he was a cop? "I don't really have a plan. I'm going to ref the game and hope someone tells me something revealing."

One side of his upper lip curled, making him look a little like a short Elvis. "I don't think that's a great plan."

She eased her sore body down onto the couch. "Well, I'm afraid it's the only one I've got."

He stared at her for a minute and then sat down beside her. Sammy, still in his bucket seat, stared up at Bob with a foolish grin. "Want me to set him free of that contraption?"

She nodded gratefully. "Thanks. I wasn't sure I could bend over to do it."

Bob effortlessly scooped Sammy up into his arms as if he'd done it a million times before. What did she know? Maybe he had.

"How big is your district?" she asked.

"Huh?" He gave her a quick befuddled glance before returning his eyes to Sammy's.

"How big is your area? How many middle schools do you cover?"

He didn't answer, and she knew that this too was a secret. Eventually, she'd learn to stop asking him questions.

"Not as many as you'd think," he said, sounding wistful.

She wondered if angels had rivalries with nearby angels, like schools did. She decided they probably didn't. "So, you want me to ask Birch some specific questions? This might be my last chance to talk to him for a while."

He'd been making googly eyes at her son, but at her question, his face fell into the gravest of expressions. "Yes, I think you should."

"Well, then, I think *you* should tell me what those questions should be."

His eyes grew wide. "How should I know?"

She didn't know why he would know. But she certainly didn't have any ideas. "Do you want me to ask him if he knows who killed Frank?" She'd been kidding, but it seemed Bob was mistaking the suggestion for a literal one.

After a long pause for consideration, he said, in complete seriousness, "I don't think we should tip our hand just yet."

Sandra didn't think so either. She wasn't even sure they had a hand to tip.

Chapter 34

Sandra beat Birch to the field. She sat in her car until she saw another person clad in fluorescent yellow climb out of a pickup. Then she swallowed four ibuprofen and climbed out of her car, trying not to wince. She made her way across the parking lot to the other official. He smiled when he saw her. Her uniform had arrived that afternoon, so she stood out in the crowd. She was officially an official.

She stuck her hand out and introduced herself. He gave it a firm shake. "Harold. Good to meet ya." He slammed the door of his truck shut and started walking.

She fell into step alongside him, wondering where Bob was. He'd said he'd meet her here, but she didn't think he'd arrived yet.

"You ready for this?" Harold asked.

"I don't think so."

He gave her a hearty laugh. "Extra points for honesty. It'll be nice to have a woman around. Us men are all about having pride, or pretending at least." He strode confidently across the field, moving with more grace than she would've guessed possible, based on his rotundness.

He called the home coach by his first name and started a long boisterous conversation with him, one which Sandra felt decidedly left out of. She stood awkwardly nearby, her arms folded across her new sports bra, which had her smashed together with a force she found both uncomfortable and comforting.

As her watch ticked toward kickoff, she grew more and more nervous. So, she nearly leapt with joy when she saw Birch crawl out of a yellow Volkswagen Beetle. A familiar face. A person who knew the rules of soccer. It was possible she'd never been so excited to see anyone ever.

He jogged toward her, wearing a big smile and pulling his yellow shirt over his head, as Harold called for captains. She returned the smile and then tried to sound confident as she shook hands with the middle school girls forming the captains' circle. As Harold checked for barrettes and earrings, she tried to calm her nerves. How hard could a junior high girls' soccer game be? She could do this.

Harold sent the girls out onto the field and then asked her which side of the field she wanted for the first half. She had no idea.

"The far side," Birch answered for her. "Let you deal with the subs while she gets her feet wet."

Oh yeah, the subs. She'd forgotten that was even a thing. Grateful for Birch's wisdom, she headed for the opposite side of the field.

Harold blew the whistle, the green team kicked the ball, and Sandra forced her sore feet to move. She'd only gone about twenty feet when the ball changed direction with a decided lack of oomph. She learned something then, something that made her happier than any Christmas morning ever had: *middle school girls were slooooow.* Nothing against them. They were precious little athletes, but they were so much slower than their male classmates, and she was over the moon. She was the biggest fan of middle school girls to ever walk the earth. She could do this. She'd found her groove. She would just tell Mike White to only give her middle school girls' games for the rest of her career. Oh, who was she kidding? She was only going to do this until she cleared

Frank's name. But until that happened, it was middle school girls all the way. The ball took a full thirty seconds to roll out of bounds, giving Sandra ample time to figure out who had touched it last and which way the ball should go as a result. She blew the whistle, pointed with her arm, and was almost having fun when a fullback fully flattened a striker for seemingly no reason at all. She audibly gasped, wondered why the ref hadn't blown the whistle, and then remembered that she was the ref. She gave a loud tweet and scowled at the bully in the green shirt. Tempted to red card her and kick her out of the sport forever, she decided to just call it a push and gave the white team a direct kick.

The green moms were most unhappy with this decision. She couldn't make out everything they were saying, but one voice rose above the rest. "Let them play, ref!" She tried to tune them out while wondering if they were right. Had she been too quick to blow the whistle? As she was wondering this, a white player elbowed a green player in the face, and the women behind her erupted. "Are you blind? Call it both ways, ref!" A few expletives reached her ears, and her jaw would have dropped open in righteous indignation if it hadn't been clamped firmly around the whistle. Now she didn't know what to do. Blow the whistle or don't blow the whistle? She wished she was on the other side, dealing with the subs.

"It's okay!"

She hadn't even realized Birch was that close to her until she heard his voice. She looked at him, her eyes wide with incredulity.

He laughed and slapped her on the back. "No, really. First one was a great call. You missed the second one, but so what? Get your head back in the game. You're doing great."

Feeling only moderately encouraged, she tried to focus. But the green moms continued to scream at her throughout the first half, and when it was time to cross to the other side, she felt like she was crossing the Jordan into the Promised Land.

Chapter 35

The second half of Sandra's first game was no better. She could no longer hear the moms. Now she could hear the coaches, and they were equally angry with her. Five minutes in, she was in tears.

A few things were going in her favor, though. First, she was sweating so profusely that no one knew those were tears streaming down her face. And second, her muscles were so warm that she wasn't in much pain.

She hadn't meant to, but she'd effectively quit blowing the whistle. She didn't realize she'd done it until Birch told her to stop being "whistle-shy." Then, she'd searched for a reason to blow it, but there hadn't been one. The game dragged on and on, and she swore to herself again that this would be the grand finale of her officiating career.

Then, after the game, as she was preparing to bolt for the safety of her minivan, the two officials flanked her and began pouring praise upon her head. At first, it didn't help, but slowly, she was persuaded that maybe she hadn't done so badly. Birch told her that it was the best first game he'd ever seen. She'd told him he was a liar. Harold, though, was more convincing. He praised her for how well she knew the rules, claiming that this was the hard part, and told her she just needed to be more confident.

She was certain that *that* would be the hard part.

Harold stooped to pick up his backpack, which was behind the scorekeepers' table. He pulled out a water bottle and took a long drink from it. That niggling voice popped into her head again: *You're supposed to be figuring out a puzzle here. You're not actually a soccer ref. You're just pretending to be one.* "I can't believe people last as long as they do in this gig," she said, trying to steer the conversation in a helpful direction. "How old was Frank? Ninety? So he had like seven decades of moms screaming at him?"

Birch stared off in the distance, pretending he hadn't heard her, but Harold guffawed. "Frank Fenton? He's been deaf as a dead dog for the last six of those decades."

She laughed too. "Maybe that's who killed him—one of those angry moms." And then right there in that second, she knew the clue that had been on the tip of her tongue since her shadow game: the water bottles!

The men started walking toward the parking lot, and she scampered to stay between them.

"Do you know how he got the poison into him?" she asked, though she was certain they had no idea.

"Can't begin to imagine," Harold said, sounding soberer.

Birch still refused to look at her, but said, "You seem awfully fixated on Frank Fenton."

Worrying she'd already blown her cover, she said, "Sorry, I guess I am. I've never knelt beside a dying man before."

Birch's eyes snapped toward her. "That was *you*?"

Oops. Consider cover blown. She nodded. "I'm afraid so."

"Sorry you had to do that," Harold said, sounding sincere.

"So you watched a man die and decided to take his job?" Birch no longer sounded friendly.

"Not exactly." That wasn't how it had happened, but she couldn't exactly tell him how it *had* happened, now could she? "Um … I've just always loved soccer," she lied, "and have been thinking about reffing for a while now." Her voice trembled with guilt. She was the worst liar in the world. Neither man said anything, their silence confirming that neither of them had bought her bologna. At the same time, they picked up their pace. They were almost to the parking lot. She was almost out of time.

"So," she said, trying to make up for the ground she had so efficiently lost, "thanks for your help. I really appreciate it."

Harold smiled down at her. "Don't mention it. Anytime. I do a lot of middle school games, so we'll be seeing a lot of each other." He pointed at Birch with his chin. "This guy will be off to bigger and better things, but don't worry, I'll have your back."

They'd reached the tar. Wordlessly, Birch split off for his Beetle, and Harold went in the opposite direction, leaving her with nothing to do but climb into her minivan. As she turned to do just that, she saw that Birch had a stuffed panda hanging from his rearview mirror. Her belly did a flop. Was that a coincidence? Had her subconscious mind seen that before? Did her dream actually mean something, and if so, *what?* Birch caught her staring at him, and she turned and scurried to her pandaless van.

She started the engine, turned up the Casting Crowns, and called out into the empty space. "Bob! Are you there?"

A voice came out of nowhere. "Be right there. Give me a sec." Though the voice clearly belonged to Bob, its distinctive quality of disembodiment made her whole body break out in gooseflesh. Had that voice been audible, or had he just telepathically communicated to her? Was she supposed to sit here with her engine running or drive away? How long was an angel sec? Could be millennia. She wanted to get home. She was suddenly starving. In fact, she wasn't sure she'd make it home. An image of the Burger King logo loomed in her mind.

Bob appeared beside her. "Great job out there!"

Relief washed over her. She didn't think he'd lie to her about her performance. In fact, she didn't think angels were allowed to lie at all, but even if they were, she didn't think Bob would. So she'd done okay. Her angel had said so.

"Where's Sammy?"

"With Ethel."

Bob beamed. "I'm so glad that's working out." The *I told you so* was implied. "So, what's up?"

Should she tell him about the pandas? She shouldn't, should she? He would think she was crazy. Maybe she was crazy.

"You sounded like you had a development," he pushed.

Oh yeah. "Do the police know how Frank was poisoned? Because I think the poison was in his water bottle."

He furrowed his brow. "I haven't heard how he was poisoned, so no, maybe they don't know. Why do you think it was in the water bottle?"

She shrugged. "I don't know, but if Mike White did it, he had to do it shortly before he died, right? Is there such a thing as a slow-acting poison?" The more she talked, the more foolish she felt. "I don't know. I was just thinking that, at each of my games so far, the school has given us free waters, and the refs drink them. So, it would be an easy way to poison a ref."

"I don't think Mike White was anywhere near that game that day."

Her stomach sank. Maybe she was wrong.

Bob looked out the windshield, squinting. "You should drive away. Those moms look angry."

Shoot. She'd forgotten all about her new fan club. She threw the van in reverse, and, without even consulting the backup cam, lurched out of her parking spot, threw the van into drive, and sped away.

"I think you might be onto something," Bob said, and Sandra felt prouder of herself than she ever had. "The water bottle makes sense. And Mike could've had someone else do it."

Once she was safely on the road and sure she wasn't being followed by a horde of soccer moms, she said, "I don't think I'm going to drink the free water anymore."

Bob snickered.

She tried to hide how pleased this made her. It was quite rewarding to make an angel laugh.

"I think we need to share your theory with the police."

Chapter 36

Sandra agreed with Bob that she should share her brilliant water bottle theory with the police. But how? And what if they already knew that? She'd sound like an idiot! So, she didn't call that night. She spent the evening rubbing peppermint oil into her sore muscles and helping her kids with homework. Then she fell asleep on the couch. So, it wasn't until four in the morning when she woke up with a crick in her neck that she started agonizing over the imminent police contact. On some level, she knew she shouldn't be scared to call them. They were the good guys, after all. But she feared she would annoy them and get into trouble for interfering. She'd never been in trouble in her life. She didn't want to start now.

Therefore, she needed to call anonymously.

Once she'd decided on that course of action, relief washed over her, and she almost fell back to sleep, but a new thought prevented that: *how?* How does one do anything anonymously in this day and age? Her bladder announced imminent danger, and she got up and crept through the darkness. As annoyed as she was to have to use the bathroom so often, she *did* do her best thinking in there—probably because that's the only time she was ever alone.

No way she could email the police. They could trace it back to her, couldn't they? But would they bother? Just what kind of budget did the state police have? Maybe she could email from a library, with an anonymous email? Yes! That was a great idea. But how would she know if they got the email? So, maybe she should call them. Did pay phones exist anymore? Should she buy a prepaid cell phone and use that? What did they call those things on *Hawaii Five-0*? Burn phones … burned phones … fire phones … whatever. She guessed it didn't matter what they were called. She would do that. If it worked for fictional Hawaiian drug lords, then it would work for her, wouldn't it? She hoped so.

With sleep now just a silly fantasy, she got up to make some coffee. She'd taken five steps in the right direction before she realized that the pain in her legs was ninety percent better. The ache that remained wasn't really pain at all— more like a faint memory that pain used to be there. She would've leapt for joy, but she feared reinjury. So, she was humming "Who You Say I Am" when Nate scared the snot out of her with a kiss on the back of her neck. She jumped what felt like a foot into the air, and her whole body broke out in goosebumps.

He laughed. "Sorry, didn't mean to startle you."

"Startle me?" she cried. "You nearly gave me a heart attack!" She tried to slow her breathing. "Don't sneak up on me like that!" *Especially when I've been crime fighting.*

He looked at her suspiciously, but then appeared to give up on figuring her out and reached into the cupboard for a coffee mug. "Why are you up so early, and why are you in such a good mood?"

"I'm up because the couch woke me up, and I'm in a good mood because I'm no longer in pain."

He opened the fridge and stared inside as if consulting a crystal ball.

"The creamer's on the right door shelf."

"Thanks." He pulled out the half and half. "That's awesome that you're feeling better. I'm impressed. Soon you'll be in such good shape you'll be running 5Ks on the weekends."

She snorted. "Hardly. Want some eggs?"

"Really? Yeah!"

Don't act like I've never made you breakfast before. Though, in truth, she hadn't in quite some time. Part of her was jittery about getting him out of the house so she could get back to crime fighting, which was ridiculous, because she still had to get the kids up and to school before she could go fire-phone-shopping.

After she'd finished scrambling, she placed his plate in front of him and kissed him on the cheek. "*Bon appétit.* I'm going to go hop in the shower before it's too late."

He chuckled. "Nah, you've still got time. Sit." He patted the table beside him. "Eat with me."

She wasn't hungry, but she sat down with her coffee, touched that he wanted to spend time with her.

"So, you think you're going to stick with this reffing gig?" He put a forkful of eggs into his mouth and then said, "You enjoying it?"

"I am." She said that because she thought that's what she was supposed to say, but once she'd spoken those two words, she realized with some shock that they were true.

Chapter 37

As soon as Sandra had Peter and Joanna delivered to school, Sammy and she took a giant step deeper into their sleuthing careers and went fire phone shopping.

With no idea where an upstanding individual should buy a fire phone, she went to Walmart, where a nice young man in a blue vest welcomed her to the technology department. This wasn't great news, as she was trying to be sneaky. She should've worn her black reffing hat. And a small matching one for Sammy. Oh well, too late now. She told the salesman that she didn't need any help, and she grabbed the eight dollar flip phone off the rack.

He met her at the checkout. "Don't you want some minutes for that?"

Minutes? She stared stupidly down at the phone.

"That's just the phone." He had the most monotone voice she'd ever heard. "You need to buy the card to activate it if you want to use it." He pointed at the thousands of cards hanging right around the phones she'd just browsed through.

"Oh, uh … yes." She headed toward the cards, but quickly became overwhelmed. There were a dozen different brands, and each brand seemed to use a different language. And though the man in the blue vest wasn't doing anything except standing behind his counter, she felt enormous pressure from his waiting. She told herself this was foolish, to just calm down, but her anxiety only grew. Then Sammy began to blat, and the top of her metaphorical teakettle started to rattle around. So, she just grabbed the shiniest card and hurried back to the counter. Once the cart was moving, Sammy stopped crying. Score one for Mom.

"Uh … this card isn't compatible with the phone."

You can't be serious. "Okay." She took a deep breath, pushing the cart away and then pulling it toward her, trying to trick Sammy into thinking he was moving. "Which card do I need?"

"One of the blue ones."

She looked. All the cards, except for the orange one she'd picked, were blue. "So, any of those blue ones will work with this phone?"

He didn't look at the cards. "Yeah. Or you can get a phone that works with this card."

She didn't trust him. "Would you mind going and getting me a card that matches this phone?" She forced a smile and glanced down at Sammy. "The baby seems to like this spot." When in doubt, use the kid.

"How many minutes do you want?"

She thought for a second. "I don't know, three?"

"Three?" He looked as if she'd just said she wanted to adopt a brontosaurus: He wasn't sure it could be done, and he wasn't even sure such a thing existed.

"Can you just get me the smallest amount possible?" she said through clenched teeth.

He left her then, and she was grateful that he didn't seem to mind going above and beyond his duty. He returned within seconds. "Is thirty days okay?"

"Yes. Thank you."

He rang her up. "Sixty-one dollars and two cents."

"Sixty-one dollars?" she repeated, too loudly. She tried to quiet down. "That was the cheapest one?"

"You didn't say the cheapest. You said the smallest amount of minutes."

It was a good thing she wasn't a real criminal. She was terrible at it. She dug through her purse, but as she feared, she only had fifty dollars and change. Tears threatened, and she didn't know what was propelling them the most, frustration or embarrassment.

"You okay?" His monotone had finally given way to variance, but he didn't sound concerned. He sounded alarmed.

"Yeah, yeah, of course. Just trying to think."

"We take credit cards."

No kidding, I never would've thought of that. But even a criminal as unskilled as herself knew that there was no point to buying a prepaid if she was going to use plastic to pay for it. She paused. Or was there?

"Do you know if the police can trace this phone back to this store?" she asked without thinking.

As his eyes widened, her cheeks warmed accordingly.

"Why, what are you going to do with this?"

"Nothing," she said quickly. "Just doing a science experiment with my son." She begged the floor to open up and swallow her. She needed to stop lying. Because it was wrong, but mostly because she was so terrible at it. "So do you know?"

He shook his head. "No, sorry. I don't know."

Every cell in her brain gave up simultaneously. "You know what? This isn't meant to be." She slid the phone and card across the counter toward him. "I'm sorry to have wasted your time." She turned, put her hands on the cart, and began to walk away.

"You wanna just use my phone?" He called after her. "If you're only going to use it for three minutes?"

She paused. Was that a good idea? She didn't know. She turned back. "Thank you for the offer." She stood thinking about it. He stood waiting for her to think. "Is it a fire phone?" she asked.

He furrowed his brow. "I don't think so." Then he picked up the eight-dollar phone from the counter, still in its package. "It's just like this phone."

She let out a long breath. This was just crazy enough to work. "Yes, thank you. Thank you, thank you, thank you." She rushed back to her favorite

Walmart employee of all time. "I'll only be a minute."

Chapter 38

It took the police only two hours to show up at her front door.

She opened it to find them standing on her porch. She recognized the officer on the right. He was Chip Buker of the giant Buker family who took up the last three pews on the right-hand side of the sanctuary. She hadn't seen him in church for a while, but she remembered he used to come occasionally. His blue uniform had made him stand out from the crowd.

He wasn't in uniform now. Both officers wore suits, making them even more intimidating.

"Are you Mrs. Provost?" Chip asked. The recognition was not mutual.

She nodded.

"I'm Detective Buker, and this is my partner, Detective Slaughter. We're with the Maine State Police. We need to ask you a few questions. May we come in?"

Why was she so nervous? She hadn't done anything wrong. She stepped back to let them in, nodding. "It didn't take you long to find me." A nervous trill of a laugh escaped her, and her cheeks got hot. "How *did* you find me?"

Without looking at her, Chip said, "You were on camera, ma'am. And someone recognized you."

Shoot. The fame of being a principal's wife. She motioned toward the living room as she shut the door behind them. "Please, make yourself comfortable." When she entered her living room behind them, she saw that there was no place for them to sit. Toys and electronics occupied every cushion in the room. She swept an arm down the couch, knocking all the mothering paraphernalia to the floor at one end. Then she motioned to the couch again. Detective Slaughter looked reluctant, as if she feared getting attacked by a soggy Cheerio— which *was* a possibility—but she did sit down, and Chip followed her lead.

Slaughter, Sandra mused. *What an apt name for a police officer.* If Sandra were a cop, she'd want to be called Detective Slaughter.

"You made an anonymous phone call," Chip said.

Was that a question?

Chip waited for Sandra to say something, and when she didn't, he asked, "Why did you choose to be anonymous?"

Why *had* she chosen to be anonymous? There were a million reasons. There was no good reason at all. "I was scared," she said quickly.

"What were you scared of?" Slaughter asked.

"Oh, I don't know. A man was murdered. Maybe I'm scared of the murderer." She hadn't meant to sound so snarky, but neither officer reacted, so maybe snark came with the territory for them.

"What made you think the poison was in the water bottle?" Chip asked.

"Was it?"

"No way to know. We don't have the water bottle."

She gasped. "And no one grabbed it as evidence?"

Chip glared at her. "Please answer the question."

She didn't want to. She was having too much fun. "But you haven't found *another* source for the poison, have you? So I'm probably right?"

"Ma'am, please."

Oh, fine. You're no fun. "I'm a soccer ref." She sat up straighter as she said this. It wasn't entirely true, not yet. She hadn't even taken the test yet, but it felt good to say it. Still, she told herself she had to concentrate on being more truthful. Either that or give up her new secret sleuthing career. So far, her amateur methodology led to far too much misrepresentation. "I was just thinking, at my last game … the schools always give us water bottles. It would be really easy to put poison in one of them."

Chip stared at her, looking contemplative. "Did you know the deceased?"

"I met him thirty seconds before he died."

Chip nodded as if he knew that. "And how long have you been a soccer ref?"

"I just started this season." No need to tell him she had only started a week ago.

"And do you have any idea who might have been angry enough with the deceased to kill him?"

Sandra shook her head, but as she did so, a face appeared in her mind. "I don't know if he would have been angry with him, because I don't know him, but have you looked at the man who was reffing with him that day? That guy would have had easy access to the water bottle."

"We can surmise who had access to the water bottle," Slaughter said, and Sandra didn't like her tone. "We're asking if you knew anyone who was angry with Mr. Fenton."

"You didn't even know the poison was *in* the water bottle, but now, a week after the fact, you're going to figure out who had access to it? Oh, please. And I just told you. *I didn't know Mr. Fenton.* So how could I know who was angry with him?"

Slaughter gave Chip an exasperated look. "I think we're done here."

Chip held up a hand to stall her. "You said that you met him thirty seconds before he died," Chip said. "Does that mean he spoke to you?"

Sandra stared at him, wondering if she should share what Frank had said. Of course she should, right? These were the police. She should tell them everything. Yet, she was feeling kind of selfish. She wanted to figure this thing out herself. And if Frank had been doing something illicit, she was reluctant to get him into trouble. Though she hardly knew the man, somehow she'd grown rather attached to him.

Chip mistook her hesitation for confusion. "You said you met him. It seems a weird phrase if all you did was watch him die."

Sandra felt a gentle nudge from inside her, telling her to be truthful. So, even though she didn't want to, she came clean. "He said to me that I had to stop White."

So much for poker faces. "And you didn't tell anyone this?" Slaughter cried.

"You're the first one to ask."

The detectives exchanged an embarrassed look.

"What do you think he meant by that?" Chip asked.

Sandra shook her head slowly. "I really don't know for sure, but the referee in charge of this district is named Mike White."

Chapter 39

Sandra sat in the minivan watching Peter's team run dribbling drills. Sammy sat behind her, chewing on his fingers. Joanna was at a friend's house having a playdate, and Sandra was lonely. And not just lonely for any old friend either. She wanted Bob. She was dying to tell him about her visit from the po-po and had even sent up a prayer requesting his presence. Of course, she prefaced her request by saying that she knew angels were busy, but if he had any spare time, she would love to see him. No emergency.

Practice was almost over when her phone rang. Excited for someone to talk to, she looked at the caller ID to see that Mike White was calling. A chill overtook her, and beads of sweat broke out on her brow. She considered ignoring the call, but of course she couldn't do that. He was her boss now. Plus, she was trying to gather information about him, so surely it didn't make sense to dodge his calls, no matter how much they creeped her out.

Maybe he's not a bad guy, she told herself. Innocent until proven guilty, right?

"Hello?" She tried to sound confident and failed.

"Good afternoon. Is this Sandra?" He sounded hesitant.

"Yes! Hello."

They exchanged pleasantries, and he asked her if she had taken her written test yet. Her stomach turned. She had been meaning to.

He read her mind. "Don't be nervous. Don't forget, it's an open-book test."

It was? "I'll do it tonight."

"Awesome. I know you'll do great."

How could he possibly know this?

"I have some games for you. How does middle school girls at Lisbon sound tomorrow?"

Excitement tickled her gut. Middle school games at Lisbon sounded quite lovely, in fact. "Sure. What time?"

"Three-thirty. I'm pairing you up with Moose again. He spoke highly of you. It sounds like you two work well together. You can carpool with him if you like. He knows where the fields are."

She stammered to come up with an excuse. Nothing against Moose, but she didn't want to carpool with any man she didn't know, or even any man she did know, save her husband. "I think I'll be running kids around on the way to the game, so I'll just get there myself. Thanks anyway."

"Okay, and before I let you go, can you do two middle school boys' games in Naples on Saturday?"

Peter opened the passenger side door and climbed in wordlessly.

She didn't even know where Naples was, exactly, only that it was far. She started to accept, nonetheless, when she remembered Fall Fest. "Oh shoot. Sorry. I can't do Saturday. I usually can, but this Saturday is Fall Fest at church." As the excuse left her lips, she thought it sounded lame, so she added, "It's a bigger deal than it sounds."

He chuckled. "I understand. Family comes first. All right then. I'll write you down for Lisbon for now. I'll assign you some more games soon, though, so keep an eye out."

"Okay, great, thanks." She hung up the phone and looked at her son. "Hi, honey. You looked great out there. Did you have fun?"

He gave her an annoyed look. "It's not supposed to be fun, Mom, not anymore."

She thought she knew what he meant, but she didn't like the sounds of it, so she feigned confusion. "What?"

"Soccer is serious business now. I'm not a little kid anymore."

She started the van, disappointed that she hadn't seen Bob. "I don't care if you're a hundred. If it's not fun, there's no point in playing."

He rolled his eyes. "I think the professionals would disagree."

She looked over her shoulder as she backed out of the parking spot. "Honey, one of my daily prayers for you is that you end up with a career that you love, a job that is so much fun you would do it for free."

He snickered. She knew he was trying to act like he was still annoyed, but she could also tell that he appreciated her sentiment. "Well, then I hope someone will pay me to play video games for the rest of my life."

"You never know." She pulled out into traffic. Why were there so many people on the road? This road didn't even go anywhere.

"We're going to Fall Fest?"

"Of course. We go every year."

"I know, but I hadn't heard you mention it this year, so I was hoping we were skipping it. You're not volunteering, are you?"

He had a point. She did usually volunteer. Guilt tried to worm its way through her brain, but she pushed it out. "I've been a little busy."

"I know. So, can we skip it?"

She was tempted by the idea. Fall Fest was not her favorite occasion. An all-day outdoor affair, when it was usually too chilly for an all-day outdoor affair. The kids all bobbed for apples and then ran around with wet hair and blue lips. Some poor sap, usually the youth pastor, sat dripping and shivering in the dunking booth. And there were always a zillion people there—an introvert's nightmare. But she also knew that Nate wouldn't want to skip it. "Sorry, honey, I think we have to do it, but you can hang out with me."

He rolled his eyes again. She wondered if his eyes ever got tired. She was pretty sure she had never been allowed to roll her eyes at her parents like that. But she rolled her eyes often enough now to make up for it. She knew where Peter had gotten the habit.

"Oh sure, that will help my social situation a lot if I hang out with my mommy all day."

She giggled. There had been many a Fall Fest when he had, in fact, hung out with his mommy all day, and gladly. But those days were over now. She missed cute little snuggly Peter, but she also really liked this version of him. "Maybe you could bring a friend from school? Then you wouldn't have to talk to the church kids." The absurdity of what she had just said was not lost on her.

"I hate to break it to you, Mom, but Fall Fest is kind of lame. I'm not sure any of my friends would want to come. Though, I have heard some girls talking about it. I guess Jack and Ethan are bringing their girlfriends."

Sandra's stomach rolled. Those kids had girlfriends? They were way too young. Did Peter have a girlfriend? Of course not. She would know if he did. She could ask him, just to make sure, but he was actually talking to her, and she knew that if she took it into awkward territory, the conversation would quickly cease. "Sorry, honey. I'm afraid we're just going to have to suck it up. It's only one day."

Chapter 40

Though Mike White had told her it was an open-book test, she couldn't bring herself to believe him. If he was a murderer, he was also probably a cheater. And besides, she wanted to prove to herself that she knew the rules. So, she squirreled herself away in her bedroom with her laptop, locked the door, and logged on. A few of the questions made zero sense, and she wrestled with those until she eventually surrendered and just chose C, grateful there was no time limit. But of those questions that *did* make sense, she got one hundred percent of them correct, leaving her with a total score of 94 out of 100. Beaming with pride, she closed the laptop and ran downstairs to tell everyone.

No one cared. Nate nodded absentmindedly, never moving his eyes from the television. She couldn't bring herself to be angry. She knew he'd had a rough day and was exhausted. She was more disappointed that Peter didn't care, and had to remind herself that he was a kid. She was supposed to be proud of his test scores, not necessarily the other way around. Of the four of them, Joanna was the most excited and gave Sandra's legs an enthusiastic congratulatory hug. Sandra knew that Joanna didn't understand what had gone right in Sandra's life, but she still appreciated the support. She and Joanna were going to have to stick together in this male-dominated family.

She sat down beside Nate and waited for commercials. Then she said, "How committed to Fall Fest are we?"

He turned toward her, his brow furrowed. "What does that mean?"

She leaned back into the cushions and exhaled slowly. "It means that we're all pretty busy, and it might be nice to just hang out and do nothing on Saturday. Plus, I got offered two games for that day, which I'll have to turn down if I do Fall Fest."

"Didn't you say reffing wouldn't interfere with family time?" She didn't have to look at him to know he was scowling at her.

"Fall Fest isn't family time, unless you count me pushing Sammy around in the stroller. Everyone else is off doing their own thing."

"I can't skip it," he said. "I'm running the pony rides."

Of course he was. "You didn't tell me that."

"Did I need to tell you that?"

She hadn't meant to start an argument. "Of course not. I just didn't realize." Now that she thought about it, she wasn't surprised. Nate never missed an opportunity to be involved in a community event. He loved seeing his students outside of school.

Sandra glanced at her oldest son and tried to convey love with her eyes, as if to say, *I tried.*

He gave her a little nod that said he knew that she had.

"You want to help your dad with the ponies?"

Gratitude vanished from Peter's face. "No!" he cried. "Mom, just drop it!"

She didn't want to drop it. She was desperate to fix it. "We can make a big deal about how we're forcing you to help, and you could act all cool and complain the whole time." She forced a laugh, as if by laughing at herself she could somehow make herself funny.

Nate gave her a confused look. "What's this?"

"Mom, I'll be fine. I'll just go to the stupid thing like everyone else." He grabbed his backpack and stomped up the stairs.

"What was that all about?"

She stared at her husband, wondering how he could be so clueless. "What was that about? If your son hates going to church because of the other kids there, why would he want to go hang out there on Saturday too?"

Understanding dawned on Nate's face, and he looked sympathetic. "I guess he doesn't have to go."

"Really?" This shocked her. "So maybe he and I could just skip it?"

Nate's frown returned. "No, I need you there."

She knew he didn't need her there at all. In fact, she could vanish and he wouldn't realize she was gone until suppertime, but she didn't see any benefit in arguing the point. "Well, we can't just leave Peter home alone."

"True." He looked thoughtful. "He needs to go too. We'll keep a close eye on him, make sure nothing bad happens."

Sandra, knowing how subtle teen bullying could be, couldn't imagine how they could do that, but she would try. She wished she had the ability to red card kids in real life, just blow her whistle, whip out that little red piece of plastic, and send the offenders home. In fact, she'd red card the parents too.

Chapter 41

The Lisbon middle school soccer field was like a back road in a Maine March: there was a pothole every six feet. Sandra was spending so much time looking at the field, making sure she didn't fall into a sinkhole, that she wasn't really watching the game. Moose mentioned this, when he stopped the clock for an injury. One of Lisbon's halfbacks had indeed fallen into a crater that was almost as big as she was.

Sandra tried to defend herself, but Moose cut her off. "Oh, I know. This field is treacherous, but we still need to watch the game. If you break an ankle, you can sue." He held his belly with both hands and laughed as if this was hysterical. "I haven't been lucky enough to break an ankle yet."

She wasn't so sure it was luck. She looked at the sky, wondering if one of Bob's tasks was keeping refs from falling into the abyss. Then she wondered why she was looking at the sky. She wasn't sure Bob even spent any time up there. If he did, she certainly couldn't picture it. And just where *had* Bob been lately? He was the worst investigative partner ever. No, that wasn't true. She'd rather work with an elusive angel than with Detective Slaughter.

She took off her hat to give her head a few seconds to cool off. She hated to do this, as she felt more exposed with her hat off. She was delighted with how much anonymity the hat granted her, even if it was mostly in her head. But right now, she needed a break from the black fabric. It was eighty-two degrees out with a hundred percent humidity—unseasonably hot for September. But this was Maine. So on Saturday, when the youth pastor needed some heat, it would be forty-six degrees with a wind chill of twenty.

The trainer helped the injured girl off the field, and the substitute trotted out into her spot. As Moose put his whistle to his lips, Sandra put her hat back on and got into position. She couldn't believe how sweaty she was. Her clothes were soaked. She'd be embarrassed, but no one would get close enough to her to know how gross she was, so it was okay.

The clock started and Sandra refocused herself and didn't let herself look at the ground. *Bob will keep me on my feet.* Once she'd stopped hyper-focusing on the holes in the field, she began to find her rhythm. She missed a few fouls, but Moose called them from the other side of the field, and the Lisbon moms seemed to be a pleasant bunch. For starters, there weren't very many of them, and those who were there were looking at their phones.

She did get hollered at once, by the away coach, but she knew she'd made the right call, so his screaming didn't affect her much. She was surprised at this. In other parts of life, having a man scream at her in public would've wreaked havoc on her emotional health.

At some point, Sandra realized she was having great fun and almost giggled in surprise. When the ball rapidly changed direction and she had to turn and sprint down the field, she felt like she was flying. She wasn't, of course. On a logical level, she knew she couldn't be going that fast. She was chasing young girls, and *they* weren't very fast, yet she felt like she was soaring. She couldn't remember the last time she had felt so free, and she didn't want the game to stop.

Then, at halftime, Moose said something about a second game, and a voice in Sandra's head suggested that maybe she should be pacing herself. "There's a second game?" she asked, breathing hard.

Moose laughed. "There sure is. There are usually two games when you have a middle school assignment. This is the seventh-grade girls. The eighth-graders play next, and you'll be surprised how much stronger and faster they are. A year makes a big difference."

Uh-oh. Sandra wasn't sure she had the energy for a second game. She put her hands on her hips, still panting. "I think I might die, even if the sinkholes don't get me."

Moose laughed again. "This humidity isn't helping. But you'll be fine. Make sure you drink your water." His sparse hair was dripping wet, and he used his sleeve to wipe some sweat from his eyes. "We can always go a lot farther than we think we can."

"You should put that on a T-shirt," she said as she trotted back across the field for the second half—without touching her free water.

Chapter 42

Moose hadn't been kidding. Eighth-grade girls *were* a lot faster than the seventh-graders had been, and Sandra decided that she was going to start a petition to ensure that the fast kids always played first.

With every step, Sandra was sure she couldn't take another, but the steps just kept coming. She dug into reserves she didn't even know were there.

And perhaps it was this exhaustion that emboldened her to hand out her first card.

An angry-looking fullback on the blue team definitely committed obstruction as she protected the ball long enough for her keeper to scoop it up, but as the keeper went for it, it squirted away from her, and white took it away and headed for the goal. For reasons Sandra couldn't imagine, the Lisbon coach went ballistic. He wanted her to call the obstruction, even though that would mean forfeiting his girls' breakaway. Almost laughing at the man, she tried to ignore him.

But he wouldn't stop. One of his strikers got a shot on goal, which she blew, and the ball went out of bounds. As blue set up for a goal kick, his screaming got louder and more obnoxious. Sandra finally allowed herself to look at him, and what she saw alarmed her. His face was as red as any face had ever been and he was jumping up and down like a toddler mid-tantrum.

Sandra knew how to deal with a toddler tantrum. She knew she had to be more stubborn than the child. She looked at Moose, asking permission with her eyes, and he gave her a slight nod.

She blew the whistle, held her arms up to stop the clock, and then headed toward him.

He stopped shouting and glared at her, his hands on his hips. He knew what was coming. A hush fell over the crowd. They knew what was coming. She couldn't even believe what she was doing, but she was going to do it, no matter what. *No way* was she going to let a toddler best her.

She stopped twenty feet short of him and took out her little black folder. Then she pulled the yellow card out and held it up in the air.

Then she restarted the game, trying not to smile when Moose winked at her.

The coach was quiet for the rest of the first half, and she steered far clear of him for halftime.

"Well done," Moose said when she trotted over to him.

"Thank you."

"I mean it. It takes most new refs a while to get up the courage to card a coach."

She was surprised to hear this. "Well, he was being a psycho."

"Yes, he was. But still, good job."

She tried not to beam with pride, but she was feeling pretty good about herself, like she was finally in control of something, and like she'd found a way to stick up for herself. It was a heady moment.

During the second half, she had to stop the clock for a different, slightly more peculiar reason.

A chubby black cat tried to join the game.

Sandra first caught sight of him out of the corner of her eye while the ball was on Moose's end of the field. He strode out onto the eighteen and then lay down in the sun. Sandra glanced at the goalkeeper, they shared a giggle together, and Sandra thought that was the end of it. She refocused on the game, figuring the cat would flee the scene as soon as the ball headed his way.

This was not the case. The cat seemed completely fearless as twenty eighth-grade girls bore down on him at full speed. Maybe he didn't see them coming? Most of them definitely did not see him there. Sandra didn't know what to do. She panicked. She couldn't stop the game for a cat, could she? But she couldn't let the cat die, could she?

She blew the whistle and stopped the clock. Everyone stopped running and stared at her. Now what? Nothing in her meager training had prepared her for this. It hadn't been on the test. It wasn't on the YouTube videos. But there everyone was, staring at her, waiting for her to move. She glanced at Moose, but he was still a hundred feet away, and though he would reach her eventually, he didn't seem to be in any hurry.

So, she approached the cat. He watched her coming, but he didn't move a muscle. Until she bent over to scoop him up. Then he leapt to his feet and sprinted a mere three feet away—just out of her grasp. A few of the girls giggled, and she thought about carding them too. But she tried to be a good sport.

Moose finally reached the action. She looked at him and mouthed, "What do we do?"

He shrugged. "I don't know."

Great. She strode toward the cat, who waited until she reached him and bent over before running away again. This was getting embarrassing, and she was losing her patience. Perhaps God was trying to humble her after her first-half pride surge. She went for the cat again, faster this time, and he scurried away, disappearing for a moment among a bunch of shin guards. "If anyone else wants to grab him, go ahead," she said.

No one moved.

She lunged for him again. This time he let out a cry that made it sound as though he were being tortured. No one had touched him. This was not funny anymore. She thought about telling all the girls to run at him at once, but he didn't run away from them—only her. Maybe she should just let them play, let him get run over.

The goalkeeper who had begun this journey with her came alongside her. "Can I try? I'm really good with cats."

Sandra nodded eagerly. The petite goalie got down on all fours and started making a clicking sound with her tongue. A few girls laughed at her, and Sandra shushed them. She crawled toward him, holding one limp hand out in front of her. Much to Sandra's shock, the cat edged toward her and then nuzzled against her fingers.

The goalkeeper let out a little grunt as she dove for the cat. He tried to dart away, but her body blocked his path as she landed beside him, nearly surrounding him with her body, and holding him to her stomach with one hand.

All the girls cheered. The crowd cheered. Even the yellow-carded coach clapped. The goalie stood up, holding the wayward feline in her arms. She looked at Sandra as if to say, "What do I do with him now?"

Sandra had no idea. She looked at Moose, but he appeared to have no idea either. They all stood around for a minute just staring at the cat. Finally, the away coach hollered, "I can have someone on my bench hold him."

Sandra glanced at the cat, who did seem content to be held. That was lucky. She nodded, and the goalie delivered the cat to the waiting coach like a maternity nurse hands off the newborn.

Sandra gave her favorite goalie ample time to return to her goal, and then she started the clock, fervently hoping she wouldn't have to stop it again. Ever.

Chapter 43

Sandra felt like a million bucks. She also felt like she might drop dead from exhaustion, or heat stroke, or both, before getting to her minivan.

But she didn't. Though her legs felt like jello, she made it to her van and climbed inside. She took off her hat, started the van, and blasted the air conditioning at her face. The air was as hot as a furnace, but the promise of the iciness to come was enough to comfort her. She took a long drink from the water bottle she'd brought from home and kept in the locked van, and then sat there panting.

She couldn't believe how much fun she'd just had. Whether or not she ever figured out who killed Frank Fenton, she thought she'd continue being a soccer official. She didn't want to give it up. She hadn't received her first paycheck yet, but she thought she'd do this for free if she had to.

She eased her van out into the slow trickle of traffic. No one was in a hurry, as the driveway to the Lisbon Middle School fields was a mile-long dirt road that sported even more potholes than their soccer field did.

But Sandra was in no hurry. She turned up the Casting Crowns and sipped on her water bottle, and by the time she reached the tar road, the air-conditioning was actually cold.

Only five minutes later, she turned it down because she caught a chill. Her wet clothes grew more uncomfortable with each mile. And with each mile, she grew more excited about getting home and stepping into a hot shower. As she was daydreaming about this hot shower and the cozy flannel pajamas that would follow, she realized with dismay that she had to go to the bathroom. She'd gotten a little carried away with the hydration. Really, going to the bathroom wasn't such a formidable task, but she hated to go anywhere in her fluorescent yellow costume, especially when it was dripping wet and plastered to her body. She drove by two gas stations that probably would have worked, but they appeared too busy. She was hoping to find one that was a bit more deserted.

And then there it was on the horizon, a small mom-and-pop shop that might not even have a bathroom. But at least there were no other cars in the driveway. She pulled in and parked right beside the door. Despite her enthusiasm for the restroom, it took her a while to climb out of the vehicle. Her legs, which had been absolute champs for four thirty-minute halves, had stiffened up during her drive. As she waited for them to cooperate, she had the strangest feeling that she was being watched. She looked around, expecting to see Bob—but she didn't.

What she did see was difficult to process. A flurry of motion and a flash of red. Someone was close to her, *too* close to her; absurdly, her first concern was how sweaty she was. But then her head exploded in a pain that didn't make sense. Something had hit her—hard. Her stomach rolled, and her knees buckled, but someone grabbed her from behind before she could fall the rest of the way to the ground.

At first, she felt gratitude. Someone had kept her from falling. But then her brain made a disturbing calculation: that person had hit her. And now that person was dragging her. She opened her mouth to scream and managed a bellow she was proud of. She tried to scream, "Fire!" but only managed a high-pitched "Fi!" before a hand clamped over her mouth. She gasped for air and tasted the saltiness of his hand, which, absurdly, made her angrier than any of this incident had thus far. A salty hand in her mouth was *gross*, and her chest filled with rage. She bit down on that nasty hand with all her might, and her attacker cried out in pain before calling her an incredibly impolite name. "If you want to live through this, you might want to be more cooperative," a voice hissed into her ear, and she knew that voice.

Oddly, this knowledge comforted her. She wasn't being kidnapped by a stranger. She was being kidnapped by a fellow soccer ref.

Chapter 44

Birch Kabouya tried to push her into the trunk of a car, and she fought like she'd never fought before. She rammed her arms out ahead, before her head could hit the bottom of the trunk. She sank her fingernails into the dirty carpet and then braced herself with her arms as she drove her right foot back like a psychotic mule. How she wished she were wearing soccer cleats! Or a stiletto.

Again, he cried out, and the pressure of his hands eased off just enough so she could flip over and kick again with her other foot. This time she brought the foot from ground toward sky and connected to a sensitive part of his body with a satisfying force. As he groaned, she screamed with all her might. She didn't bother with the fire ruse this time; she just let out a primal wail from the core of her being. As she screamed, she feared that most of the sound was being trapped by the trunk and she scrambled to get her head back out into the open air. Unfortunately, her last flip and kick had left her terribly off balance, and as she struggled to get back in control of her body, he put one hand on the top of her sweaty head, grabbed her leg with the other, and then forced the rest of her small body into the trunk. She grabbed his dreadlocks with one hand, not getting as many of them as she wanted, and tried to yank herself back out of the trunk, like she was falling off a cliff and his hair was her safety line.

One strong punch to her stomach ended this attempt. Suddenly, her only mission in life was to breathe again, and as she gasped for air, he tucked her one free foot into the trunk and slammed it shut. As she tried to catch her breath, her fingers frantically searched the trunk, looking for the little emergency release that would set her free. On some level, she knew that any kidnapper worth his salt would have removed this release in advance, but this wasn't his car, so maybe he hadn't thought of it. Besides, was Birch the sharpest knife in the drawer? He had, after all, abducted her in broad daylight in a public place. She vowed to herself that from now on, she would only pee at the busiest gas stations she could find. And as her fingers searched the darkness, and as she tried to catch her breath, she heard Birch on his

Bluetooth connection. "Yeah, I got her. Meet you at the camp."

Oh good. They were going to have a soccer ref meeting at a camp. The car picked up speed, and she tried to relax, tried to think. There must be a way out of this, must be something she could do.

Oh! Duh! Why hadn't she prayed yet? She squeezed her eyes shut and begged for rescue. "Please, God, don't let me die. My babies need me. Please get me out of this. Please send Bob. Actually, wait. If you have better angels available, please send them. I mean, nothing against Bob, but I'm not sure he's much of a fighter."

Tears threatened to spill as she prayed, and she wondered why she was fighting them. Then, after a while, she didn't, and they poured out of her eyes and onto the floor of her least-favorite person's borrowed trunk.

How far are we going? With each passing mile, her fear of dying decreased, and her fear of peeing in her pants increased. Not that she would mind soiling Birch's borrowed trunk. It was the least she could do. But she didn't want to pee in her pants. That would be gross and embarrassing. And eventually, she would be rescued, and wanted to retain her dignity for that moment.

She took a deep breath and then said, as loudly as she dared, "Sorry to bother you, Birch, but I *really* need to go to the bathroom."

No response. Had he heard her? She waited a second and then tried again. "I promise to behave. I just really need to go." And there she was, lying again. "I can go anywhere. Just let me out in the woods somewhere." She didn't know where they were, but this was Maine, so there were woods nearby.

"We're almost there."

Aha! He had heard her! This was good, right? She should get him talking. She'd read somewhere that hostages should humanize themselves, right? She needed to form a relationship with Birch.

"How much farther?"

"Shut up!"

Okay, maybe he didn't want her to be humanized. She considered her words carefully. "When women have babies, their bladders get pretty pathetic."

Nothing from the front.

"And I've had three."

Still nothing.

"I was stopping at that store because I had to use the restroom, and I'd already been holding it for quite a while by that point."

Infuriating silence.

"I really don't want to pee in your trunk."

Brakes. He didn't say anything, but brakes were even better than words. The car didn't stop, but he had definitely slowed down.

"Do *not* pee in this car!"

"I don't *want* to pee in your car, Birch! That's why I'm asking you to pull over."

"Just hold it!" He sounded terrified. "We're almost there!"

She laid her head back and tried to relax, wondering if he was scared of her having an accident or scared of being late for whomever they were meeting at the camp.

Chapter 45

The trunk opened, and brilliant sunshine blinded her. She tried to look around, but all she could see was a dark shadow of Birch, surrounded by bright light—like a halo. She considered telling him she was on friendly terms with an angel of the Lord, just to mess with him, but first things first. "Seriously, Birch, all that matters right now is my bladder. I don't even care if you kill me at this point. Just let me pee first."

"Let's go," he said and roughly grabbed her arm. Apparently, he was going to pull her out of the trunk by her elbow and let her land on her butt.

She focused on getting her feet out in front of her, aware that she was missing out on more kicking opportunities; it didn't matter. She hadn't been joking about her priorities. It felt blessedly cool outside of that blasted trunk, even though it was still hotter than the blazes. Her eyes adjusting, she saw that they were at a decrepit camp beside a lake or pond. She didn't recognize any of it. "Where are we?"

He pushed her toward the shack. "There's a bathroom inside. Hurry up. He'll be here soon."

She took off running, half expecting the camp to be locked. It wasn't. She rushed inside, found the bathroom, and then experienced the strongest relief of her life.

"Hurry up!" he barked from the other side of the thin door, as if his lips were pressed against the plywood, before she'd even finished her business.

"I'm going as fast as I can! You don't have to eavesdrop!"

As she finished, the fear of peeing her pants dissipated and was replaced by the fear of dying. She looked around the tiny bathroom for an escape route that didn't exist. There was only one window, and it was so tiny she doubted she could've pushed Joanna through it. Then she looked around for a weapon. But there was nothing. If there'd been a mirror, she would've tried to break it and grab a shard of glass. But there was no mirror.

"Don't make me come in there and get you," he growled.

She closed her eyes, said another prayer, and flushed the toilet. Then she reached for the door handle. That's when she saw a nail sticking out of the wall. It was deeply, but not entirely, embedded. Could she pull it out? She doubted it. But she would try. She reached up, pinched it between her thumb and finger, and pulled.

Nothing.

"Sandra, I'm not kidding around here!"

"Just a second!" she snapped. She frantically wiggled the nail back and forth, and it moved! Not much, but it had moved! With more force this time, she pushed the nail away from her and pulled it back again as she looked around the room for something harder to push with, but there was nothing in this stupid little room except the toilet.

The toilet! She ripped the top of the tank off and then whirled around to push the giant chunk of porcelain against the side of the nail. She felt the nail give and reached up to yank it out.

Then she stared at it, as if she couldn't believe it was really in her hand. But it was.

Now, what was she going to do with it? Stab him in the eye and run? Was she even capable of such a thing? Images of her children flashed through her mind, and she realized that yes, indeed, she was capable of such a thing. She tucked the nail into her pocket, suddenly grateful that reffing shorts came with a thousand pockets. Birch wasn't likely to check them all. She had turned to replace the toilet tank cover when she thought better.

She looked down at the odd-shaped object in her hands. This, in itself, was a weapon, wasn't it?

"That's it! You've got three seconds or I'm knocking that door down!"

Knock the door down? Why? The door didn't have a lock on it. Couldn't he just use the handle? His voice sounded farther away, as if he'd backed up to get a running start. Was he going to kick the door down? Frantic, she tried to decide where to stand. There really wasn't a spot that wasn't directly in front of the door.

The toilet! She had to stand on the toilet! This toilet just kept getting handier and handier. Trying to be quiet, she climbed up onto the toilet and got ready to leap. She couldn't even believe what she, Sandra Provost, was about to do. *Could* she even do it? She was a housewife, for crying out loud. No. She was more than that. She was a daughter of the God of the universe and she was a soccer ref. She could do this. She lifted the toilet tank cover up over her head, and then bent her knees and waited.

The man with the ridiculous first name began to count. "One … two …"

Chapter 46

"Three!" Birch crashed through the door, and Sandra realized in the blur that he hadn't kicked the door down; he had lowered his shoulder and driven through it headfirst.

What a fantastic stroke of luck. Not realizing that she was going to let out a crazy high-pitched banshee war-wail, she did, as she leapt off the toilet and brought the chunk of porcelain down on Birch's head. Even leaping off a toilet, she barely had any height advantage. His eyes widened in realization of what was about to happen, and he tried to dodge the blow, but there was nowhere to go. His arms flew up to block it, and he managed to get one hand between the weapon and his noggin, but the blow was still significant.

The tall, muscular man with the large knees crumpled to the floor, and Sandra, worried that she'd actually killed him, fell on top of him in a mess of limbs. She scrambled to her feet and stared down at him in wonder. Her crazy plan had actually worked. His chest was moving. He probably wasn't dead. All the dreadlocks must've cushioned the impact.

Now what should she do? She should tie him up, right? So he couldn't chase her? But did she want to take the time? Mike White was coming, right? Or at least *someone* was?

The sound of an approaching engine made the decision for her. She started for the door, but then, out of the corner of her eye, saw that there was a back door, and she turned to head that way. It was locked, and her frantic fingers spent precious seconds trying to unlock it, but then she was out the door and running into the woods. She winced as sticks broke beneath her feet. She shouldn't be making so much noise, but she couldn't help it. She ran as fast as she could, so glad she'd been training for this for the last few weeks, and when she heard a man bellow something indistinguishable behind her, she ran even faster.

She stayed near the shoreline, in part because the going was easier, and in part because she hoped to stumble upon another camp. She hoped to find one with a Good Samaritan, a phone, or both. She ran and ran, and despite the adrenaline, her legs grew tired. With dismay, she realized she'd been going uphill for a while, and she looked to her left to see that the water was quite a ways below her now. Her chest burned for air, and her muscles were cramping. Praying "God, save me" over and over, she slowed her run to a walk and then to a slow walk. She bent over and tried to breathe quietly, tried to listen for the sounds of approaching madmen. But there was nothing.

Maybe they hadn't followed her.

Yeah, right. They had followed her. This thought got her moving again, and she began to walk, and then, when the earth sloped downhill again, she began to run. And it was then that her toe caught on an exposed root, and inertia carried the top half of her toward the ground. She put her hands out to brace herself, and they did their job. With relief, she realized she wasn't injured. But that relief was quickly overwhelmed by the realization that she was still falling. Only it was more like rolling. Rolling down the hill toward the water. She let out a little cry, which she instantly regretted, and her fingers clawed at the ground, trying to find something to grab.

And then there was nothing. Nothing to grab, and no ground beneath her. She was free-falling. *Lord, let the water be deep*, she thought as she crashed through the surface with a terrific splash.

It was deep. *Thank you, Father.* It was also *freezing* cold. Today's impromptu heat wave had done nothing to heat this mystery lake up, and as Sandra burst back up through the surface, she immediately swam for shore. She wasn't a strong swimmer, but she put her face in the water and kicked for all she was worth, sure she was going faster than she ever had.

Her hand struck the bottom, and she scrambled to her feet, wiping the water from her eyes as she staggered onto the shore. *At least I'm not sweaty anymore*, she thought and actually managed to smile at the thought.

"What's so funny?" a gravelly voice asked, and Sandra stopped smiling.

Chapter 47

Sandra looked up into the angry eyes of a man holding a gun in his right hand, his arm outstretched toward her. Beside him stood the even angrier Birch. Oh good, so he wasn't dead. What a relief. Her hands slid down her shorts, and she was relieved to find that the nail hadn't floated out during her impromptu autumn dip.

The man holding the gun looked familiar, and at first, she couldn't place him. Then he said, "You sure are a lot of trouble," and she recognized his voice. He was the ref who'd been working with Frank when he'd died.

"It was you," she said, not knowing if she'd said it out loud.

The man laughed. "What? What was me?"

In that moment, Sandra knew that she was going to die, and she wasn't even that sad about it. She was mostly just irritated. She said a silent prayer for her children. Then, "If you're going to kill me, at least tell me why you did it."

"I'm not going to kill you," he said sibilantly. "You've just decided that being a housewife wasn't enough for you. So you've hopped a bus to Vegas. We've already moved your car to the bus station."

Sandra laughed, but her face didn't have the energy to smile. "No one will ever believe that. I *love* being a housewife, you idiot. I *love* my husband, my children, my home. You're *never* going to get away with this."

She wasn't sure, but she thought doubt flickered across his face.

"Well, we're at least going to try." He cocked his gun. "You should've stayed out of this. You should've just focused on your cozy little life you love so much. This didn't have to happen—"

"What are you talking about?" she cried. "I didn't stick my nose into anyth—"

"You went to the police!" he nearly shouted. "You don't think we know that you're the reason they've hauled Mike in?"

Oh? Well, there was some good news, at least.

"Why'd you kill Frank Fenton?" she asked, impressed with the strength of her voice.

The man whose name she didn't know tipped his head to the side. "Frank was *also* sticking his nose where it didn't belong. It's a dangerous hobby."

She was suddenly desperately tired of conversing with this person. She looked at Birch. "I'm glad I didn't kill you. I was worried there for a second."

He nodded, not looking convinced. In fact, he looked a little scared of her. "I'm sorry we have to kill you. I'm really not a murderer, but you've left us no choice."

"Us?" She raised an eyebrow. The wind blew, and a chill overtook her. "How many of you are in on this?"

Birch shook his head. "Just a few."

She looked at the gun. "Birch, I get that I'm going to die. So please tell me what I'm dying for. Is that too much to ask?"

Birch started to talk, and the man with the gun told him to shut up. "Do you want Dad to kill you too?"

Her eyes snapped to his face. "Dad? Who's Dad?"

He rolled his eyes, and her heart ached for Peter. How she wanted to hug him one last time and tell him how proud she was of him. Her eyes filled with tears.

"Mike is his father," Birch said, "and Mike is a dangerous dude. I'm not mixed up in any of it except for the reffing, but I do what Mike tells me to do, because, like I said, he's a dangerous dude. He told me to grab you, so I did." His hand drifted to the top of his head. "I never dreamed you could be so much trouble."

"I said, *shut up!*" Junior White said.

"What do you mean, *mixed up in reffing?*" She shoved her hands in her pocket and curled her fingers around the nail. Absurd, she knew, to try to go up against a handgun with a nail, but it was all she had.

"We're on the take," Junior White said. "People pay big bucks to fix the games."

She laughed so suddenly that she snorted. This caused her to inhale some of the water she hadn't realized was still lurking in her nose, and she began to cough. For one absurd second, she wondered if she was going to drown right then and there, removing the necessity of shooting her.

Buying a middle school soccer ref? That was the craziest thing she'd ever heard. "Who pays big bucks to fix a middle school soccer game?"

she managed, while she tried to stop hacking up pond water.

"No one, you moron," Junior White spat. "We're *high school* refs, and you'd better believe the good teams pay."

If they were that good, they wouldn't have to pay. She decided it wouldn't be wise to point that out.

"It's not much money, really," Birch said. She pulled her eyes away from the gun to look at him. "And we don't do it often, but Frank found out and was going to turn us in, but Mike couldn't allow that because he's got a bunch of other—"

"Will you *shut up!*" Junior hissed.

Your dad must be so proud.

"What difference does it make? You're going to kill her, aren't you?" Though he'd stuffed her in a trunk, and though she'd beaten him half to death with a toilet, it appeared that Birch was having doubts about murdering her. She found this sentiment refreshing.

Junior stared at him for what felt like a long time. "Good thing I got here when I did, Kabouya"—

It took Sandra a moment to remember what that word meant.

—"'cause it sounds like you're losing your nerve." He returned his attention to her, and she didn't like what she saw in his eyes. Because she saw nothing. His eyes were cold and empty, and she knew her time was up.

Again, without realizing she was about to sound a war cry, she let it rip, and pulling the nail out of her pocket as she went, she charged at the man with the gun. His eyes widened with surprise, and then his hand twitched. She thought she was seeing him pull the trigger, but as she reached him, she saw that his hand was trembling, and he was staring at it as if he'd never seen his own hand before. Then his whole arm began to tremble; he now only had a loose grip on his weapon.

"What the ..." he said to himself.

Fully engaged in whatever was happening to his hand, she held off on stabbing him in the eye.

Then the gun fell out of his hand completely and landed in the soft dirt by his feet.

"What's wrong?" Birch asked.

"I don't know!" Junior wrapped his left hand around his right wrist. "Something's wrong with my hand."

She was fascinated, but her desire to survive overpowered her curiosity. She grabbed the gun out of the dirt and took off running.

"Go after her!" Junior cried.

"Why don't you?" Birch cried right back.

"I can't get my feet to move!"

Sandra's feet were moving, and they were moving fast. Despite the fact that her sneakers felt like soggy clown shoes, making a *splat* sound every time one of them hit the earth, she was setting speed records, she was sure of it. And this time she was running *away* from the lake. She came around a large pile of brambles and almost smacked directly into Bob. She let out a little screech, which she cut short so that she could snap, "Where have you been?"

Chapter 48

Bob looked offended. "Who do you think made him drop the gun?" He glanced furtively behind her. "Come on, this way." He gently pulled her in the opposite direction. She was so relieved to see him that she started weeping. He walked, and she thought about telling him to run, but she was exhausted and besides, she thought she should let the angel be in charge.

In less than a minute, they stepped into a small clearing, and Sandra looked up at a weather-worn cottage. "They're believers," Bob said. "Don't be scared." He took her by the hand and half-led, half-dragged her up the steps to their front door. He didn't even knock; he just went in as if he owned the place, quickly shutting the door behind him.

A man looked up from the Bible in his lap. "Can I help you?"

"Yes," Bob said. "Could we use your phone? It's an emergency."

"Of course!" The man looked out the window. "Is someone following you?"

"Don't worry. They won't come here."

Sandra wondered how he could know that, but somehow trusted that he did. Bob thanked the kind gentleman and took the phone from his outstretched hand. He punched in a number and then handed the phone to Sandra. She made no move to take it.

"It's Detective Buker," he whispered, pushing the phone into her arm. "Go ahead, it has to be you."

She heard Chip answer, and she grudgingly took the phone. "Hi, Chip. This is Sandra Provost, the soccer ref." Even under the circumstances, she enjoyed saying that. "I'm not sure where to start, but we need help—"

Bob shook his head frantically.

"*I* need help," she corrected. "I'm at …" She looked at the phone's owner, who had now stood up, his brow etched with worry. "What's your address?" she whispered.

He gave it to her willingly, and she repeated it to Chip. "A man named Birch beat me up and shoved me into his trunk, and then another man, I don't know his name, but I've been calling him Junior in my head, well, he tried to shoot me, but I got his gun, and I still have it." She looked down at the gun in her hand. "But they're still after me. They say Mike White sent them." Before she could even finish that sentence, he talked over her to tell her units were on the way. She realized that her whole body was shaking, and she looked at the phone owner. "Can I sit down?"

"Of course, of course!" he rushed to say and guided her toward the couch, which she collapsed onto.

"Stay with me, Sandra. We're on our way."

"Sorry … I'm all wet," she said, only vaguely aware of how peculiar she sounded. This was the softest couch in the history of couches. She'd never been so in love with a couch.

"Would you like some coffee? Hot cocoa?"

At the same time, Chip asked, "Are you hurt? Do you need an ambulance?"

She didn't know whom to answer and was overwhelmed. She shook her head at both of them. "I don't think so. And water would be great." For just a second, she thought, *no, shouldn't drink water, then you'll just have to go to the bathroom again*, but then her logical brain kicked in. That would be an okay thing now. For the rest of her life, it should be fairly easy to get to a bathroom.

The man returned with a bottle of water, which she snatched out of his hand and then drank from greedily. She hadn't realized how thirsty she was. It was no wonder. She'd exercised more today than she had in her entire life. Then he draped a blanket over her the best he could while she continued to hold the phone to her ear. She didn't know why she was doing this. "Can I call my family?" she said into the phone.

"Stay on the line with me. Detective Slaughter has already called your husband. We'll take you to your family as soon as we—"

"Oh no!" she cried, and the couch-owner jumped. "You probably scared them to death!" She realized she was whining, but couldn't help it. "Someone named Slaughter calls him and tells him I'm being chased by a murderer? Are you nuts?"

Chip didn't answer, and Sandra was glad for it. She didn't want to talk to Chip anymore. She leaned her head back and closed her eyes. As the seconds ticked by, the phone got heavier and began to slide away from her ear, and she let it. Before it hit the couch, Bob caught it and ended the call.

Sandra fought to stay awake, but she knew she was losing the battle. Just before she nodded off, Bob whispered into her ear, "You did great. We're definitely going to be able to clear Frank's name."

Without opening her eyes, she tried to smile, but she didn't know if her lips obeyed the command.

"Thanks for your help," he said. "You might not see me again, but it's been a pleasure."

"No, wait!" Her eyes popped open, and she grabbed his arms. "I need one more thing from you."

He frowned. "What?"

She leaned toward his ear and whispered her request.

He scrunched up one side of his face. "That's not really what I do."

"Then talk to the angel who does it," she said, and then felt she was being too demanding. "Please?"

He nodded. "I'll make it happen."

Well beyond pleased, Sandra allowed herself to drift off to sleep. As she did, she thought she heard Bob say, "I'm an angel of the Lord. When the police get here, do not mention me. I was never here."

Later, looking back on this memory, she would swear she'd seen the man agree, but that didn't seem plausible. In her memory, he hadn't even seemed surprised. He'd acted as though he encountered angels all the time.

Surely, she was misremembering that part of her adventure. Perhaps she'd dreamed that bit.

Chapter 49

The ER doc diagnosed Sandra with dehydration.

"I'd better not get a bill for this. I could've told you that I was dehydrated." She was certain that she *would* get a bill, but she didn't mind. She was happy to be alive.

He told her that he wanted to keep her for a few hours, just for observation, and to get some fluids into her, but that she could go home after she got some rest. She didn't argue with that. She'd never been so tired in her whole life. In fact, she didn't know it was possible to be as tired as she was and still be awake.

She wasn't awake for long. Despite the bright lights and shouts and alarms of the ER, she conked off as soon as her head hit the pillow, and she wasn't pleased when Detective Chip and Detective Slaughter woke her up.

"What?" she said, her voice thick with sleep.

"Sorry to disturb you, but we've got a few questions." He asked them, and she answered them to the best of her ability. Chip enjoyed a good belly laugh when she described her toilet tank cover maneuver, and she found that rewarding. Even Slaughter curled up one corner of her mouth.

At one point, Chip said, "You're lucky you got away when you did."

"I don't feel all that lucky."

"No?" Chip raised an eyebrow. "Didn't you just tell me that Wilfredo abruptly dropped his gun?"

"Wilfredo? Who on earth is that?"

Chip smirked. "Mike's son."

"Oh." She thought Junior was a better fit. "Yes, he just dropped it." She wished she could tell him more, but she knew she wasn't supposed to. "I think he had a seizure or something."

"Or something," Slaughter repeated.

"What did Mike do?" Sandra asked. Then she realized that was a bit ambiguous. "I mean, other than taking money to fix high school soccer games. I'm assuming he was involved in larger crimes?"

"He sure was. He fixed college games too." Chip laughed at his own joke. Then he added, "He was mostly into drug trafficking, but we're finding evidence of all sorts of related crimes.

There's evidence to suggest he's already killed some people."

Sandra's breath caught. That *was* scary. "That explains why he owns a funeral home. How convenient ... I wonder why he was a soccer ref at all. Sounds like he had enough other stuff to keep him busy."

"According to his son, he really loves soccer."

Even bad guys had to have hobbies. "Has anyone told Frank's widow, Isabelle? She should know that Mike's been caught."

"I don't know if that's happened, but we'll make sure that it does."

"And there's no evidence that Frank was mixed up in any of this, right?"

Chip shook his head. "No, why? Do you think he was?"

"No, no," Sandra said quickly. "But someone broke into Frank's house. Really trashed the place looking for something. I think Isabelle was a little worried that Frank had crossed over to the dark side."

"We are aware of the break-in," Chip said.

"You are? I didn't think Isabelle wanted to report it."

"She didn't. Frank's son did. Apparently, Mike thought Frank had some evidence. According to Wilfredo, Frank gave Mike a week to turn himself in and resign or he was going to blow the whistle on his scam—"

"The *reffing* scam?"

"Yep. Apparently, that's all Frank knew about. But if Frank reported that one relatively small crime, and the police got to poking around in Mike's affairs, imagine what they would've uncovered. Mike couldn't have that."

"So he had his son poison him?"

"Yep. Gave them a game together and told Wilfredo to take care of it." Chip shook his head, disgusted.

"Make sure Isabelle knows all this, okay? It's important that she knows what a good man her husband was."

Chip lowered his notepad and looked at Sandra curiously. "You seem to be excessively involved in this whole thing, Mrs. Provost. It's almost like you were trying to do some amateur investigating." He raised his voice at the end of his sentence.

Was that a question? If it was, was she supposed to answer it? She chose not to.

"If that was the case," Chip said slowly, "I hope you've learned how dangerous that can be."

She nodded enthusiastically. "Absolutely. I'm all done getting stuffed into trunks."

"Good. That's good to hear." Chip turned to go. "You take care of yourself, Mrs. Provost. Feel better soon."

"But I did sort of help, didn't I?"

Chip chuckled, but he didn't give her the satisfaction of turning around.

Chapter 50

As Sandra came through a wide door that opened onto the waiting room, her family assaulted her with hugs. They almost knocked her over backward, and she'd barely regained her balance before Nate's lips were on hers. She let him kiss her and then tried to pull away, but he wouldn't let her. He gently grabbed the back of her head and pushed his lips against hers. She stopped trying to get away and let him kiss her. After all, she couldn't remember the last time he'd kissed her like that.

"Enough, Dad!" Peter said, and Nate pulled away, laughing.

"Sorry, son, but I'm so in love with this woman, and I can't believe we almost lost her."

Her cheeks got hot. "You didn't almost lose me," she said, feeling sheepish.

"Well, still, I'm never letting you out of my sight again," he said, and squeezed her hand.

"Can we go home?" Sandra asked.

"Yes!" Nate declared and headed for the door. "The police say you're perfectly safe. In fact, one of the officers who caught the kidnapper says he's a friend of yours. I guess you guys ref together?"

Huh? Had all this turmoil affected her memory? "I don't know who you mean."

"I can't remember his name, but his voice sounded just like that cop from *Everybody Loves Raymond.*"

Sandra laughed. "Oh, yeah, that guy. I'm not so sure we're friends."

"Oh, okay, well, you're famous now, so everyone wants to be your friend. Anyway, he told me that they caught both men."

"*Both* men? Weren't there three of them?"

"Right. They already had the ringleader."

Oh yeah, right, thanks to my not-so-anonymous phone tip.

Nate was still talking, processing out loud. "… unbelievable. Mike seemed like such a stand-up guy. Not that I knew him well, but what I did know of him sure had me fooled."

"He had everyone fooled." *Except me*, but she left that last part out of the spoken conversation.

"And they found the other two goons still out in the woods looking for you."

"Are they hurt?" Sandra asked.

Nate stopped walking and looked at her. "Are you seriously concerned about their welfare? You are such a woman of God!" He kissed her again.

"Dad, seriously! Stop!"

Sandra smiled at Peter and ran her hand over his head. She wasn't *truly* concerned for their welfare. She was just curious if Junior's angel-induced injuries had vanished just as quickly as they'd been inflicted. "Have you heard their names?"

Nate knit his brow together.

"The criminals. I just thought it was funny that one of them was named—"

"Wilfredo!" Peter piped up. "I remember because it made me want Alfredo sauce."

"Oh-ma-ga*w*sh!" Sandra erupted, and they all jumped. "Alfredo sounds *amazing!* Can we get Italian takeout on the way home?"

Joanna's eyes grew wide. Mom never suggested takeout.

"Sure, sweetheart," Nate said, "whatever you want."

"Great. Get an extra order of breadsticks, please." Sandra didn't know how long this outpouring of affection would last, but she was going to enjoy every second of it. Maybe she should get kidnapped more often.

Nah. She didn't want to do that ever again.

They stepped out of the hospital, and Peter slid his hand into hers. "I'm proud of you, Mom. You're such a rebel."

Sandra laughed. "Thanks, honey."

"Seriously. The cops said you beat the guy up with part of a toilet."

She laughed and reached into her pocket to see if the nail was still there. It was. She thought maybe she'd put it in her jewelry box when she got home. She didn't know why, but she wanted this keepsake.

Nate opened the passenger side door for her and helped her into the vehicle. She accepted his help, even though she found it a little over-the-top. She was also finding that it gave her some butterflies in her stomach, butterflies that either hadn't been there for a while, or had suddenly woken up from a long slumber.

"I'm so, so happy to see all of you, but I'm also *super* tired. So, let's eat and then I'm going to lie on the couch and fall asleep. You're all welcome to cuddle me as I do so, but just don't be offended when I snore."

They all laughed. This was another new thing. They usually didn't find her all that funny.

"You know, guys, you might give me a complex."

"What?" Nate asked, his brow etched with concern. He was looking into her eyes, waiting for what she'd say next. She couldn't remember the last time he'd done that.

"Well, it's just that, I do heroic things all the time. I drive everybody everywhere and am never late for anything even when I've got to be in three places at once. I get grass stains out of whites, and I cook amazing meals for like three dollars a pop. And now you guys are all impressed because I thumped a guy with a toilet."

Joanna giggled. "You're funny, Mommy."

Nate leaned across the van and kissed her gently. Then he caressed her cheek as he said, "You've always been my hero for all those things. But I took you for granted, and I'm sorry. I won't let that happen again."

Chapter 51

It was the worst Fall Fest ever. While Sandra enjoyed having her family fawn all over her, she wasn't so keen to have the entire town do it. She suspected people had turned out for the festival just to get to talk to the local celebrity. She couldn't wait for the next dramatic event, so that people would forget all about her.

She was grateful that Nate had found someone else to facilitate the pony rides, so that he could stick with her. The two of them strolled around the grounds with Sammy, and Nate interfered whenever anyone trapped them for too long or asked too many annoying questions. "Did you think you were going to die?" "How did you ever allow yourself to get kidnapped in the first place?" "Why didn't you just press your panic button?" On and on it went, and Sandra would have left the Fall Fest by now if not for the small favor she'd asked of her favorite angel.

It hadn't been granted yet.

She was trying to be patient.

Though Nate didn't know it, their haphazard strolling route had really been a loose tail of

Peter's movements—except for that brief detour to support Ethel's whoopie pie booth. After that delightful distraction, Sandra and her stomachache had steered them back onto Peter's trail. So far, he'd wandered around the festival alone. Apparently, Sandra's celebrity status did not extend to her children, and for that, she was grateful.

A gaga pit was set up next to the bobbing for apples pool. They didn't have enough players, and one of the boys waved Peter over. Sandra didn't know why they didn't just draw from the gaggle of girls standing around the perimeter giggling. Apparently, for now, gaga was an all-male sport.

Sandra watched closely while pretending she wasn't watching at all. To the best of her recollection, gaga was not Peter's favorite game. But as she watched, boy after boy got knocked out of the round until it was just Peter and Ethan left standing in the pit. For the first time, Sandra wondered if Peter was accomplishing this success on his own power.

Then Peter wound up and delivered the ball with such force that Sandra knew divine intervention was in play. The ball traveled so fast that Ethan didn't have a prayer of getting out of the way, and it smacked him squarely in both shins.

He cried out in surprise, and then his face darkened in anger. He jammed one finger into the air and made a circle. "Rematch!" he cried, and everyone hopped back into the ring.

But Ethan fared no better in the second match, and one by one, the girls started to cheer for Peter instead of for him. The more frustrated he got, the worse he played. It took all the willpower Sandra could muster not to beam with pride. Instead, she forced herself to hang back and secretly gloat from afar. She and Sammy sat on a nearby swing set and silently cheered Peter on, while he wiped the ground with them in the second round and then again in the third. After three losses, Ethan no longer wanted to play and stormed off for the basketball court.

Sandra understood his thinking. Ethan excelled in basketball, so was going to where he felt most comfortable. He looked over his shoulder, obviously expecting all of his cronies to follow him, but no one did. "Hey!" he hollered. "Get over here. We're playing basketball now!"

Jack hustled after him, and the rest of them followed in a trickle. At first, Peter showed no interest in playing basketball, and Sandra couldn't blame him. Basketball was certainly not his thing. He had never shown any interest or ability. But the pretty girls were pulling on each of his arms, and grudgingly, he followed them to the court.

Ethan wound the ball at his chest. "Check."

It was evident that Peter did not know what this word meant. He looked around, stupefied. Sandra didn't know what it meant either.

"Give me the ball back, doofus!"

"What is going on?" Nate asked, apparently noticing for the first time that his son was involved in some social drama.

"Not sure," Sandra said, even though she had a pretty good idea. "Let's go check it out." She tried not to look overeager as she tucked Sammy back into his stroller and headed for a spot closer to the basketball court.

By the time she got there, the game was well underway. Someone threw Peter the ball, and though he bobbled it, he then got control, pivoted toward the hoop, and shot the ball. Sandra was no expert, but it sure looked like textbook form.

Swish. Nothing but net.

Sandra failed to hold back her triumphant laugh, but none of the kids noticed. All the girls squealed and clapped. She could almost see the smoke rolling out of Ethan's ears.

Everything that Peter threw up went through the hoop. He still couldn't dribble, pass, or play defense, but boy could he shoot. Sandra glanced at the enraptured looks on the girls' faces and realized with horror that she might've gone too far with her maternal interference. Peter might not get out of this without a girlfriend. But it was too late to stop the train. Peter had social momentum, and there was no slowing him down. Even Jack was starting to verbally kiss his butt.

Will he still be able to shoot tomorrow? she asked God, not expecting an answer.

But clear as day, she heard Bob's voice. "He will be, but he won't want to."

"This isn't the church angel's doing, is it?" she asked softly.

"Huh?" Her husband was staring at her, but she ignored him. She was listening intently for Bob's voice.

"Nope, this one is all me. I figured I owed you."

She smiled, sure her heart had never been so full. "We make a good team," she said to Bob.

"I know," Nate said, and she realized that this too was true. And even though Sammy started to bellow, she savored the moment, vowing to be equally grateful for every moment of her life from now on.

More Large Print Books
by Robin Merrill

Wing and a Prayer Mysteries
The Showstopper
The Pinch Runner

Gertrude, Gumshoe Cozy Mystery Series
Introducing Gertrude, Gumshoe
Gertrude, Gumshoe: Murder at Goodwill
Gertrude, Gumshoe and the VardSale Villain
Gertrude, Gumshoe: Slam Is Murder
Gertrude, Gumshoe: Gunslinger City
Gertrude, Gumshoe and the Clearwater Curse

Shelter Trilogy
Shelter
Daniel
Revival

Piercehaven Trilogy
Piercehaven
Windmills
Trespass

Robin Merrill also writes sweet romance as Penelope Spark:
The Billionaire's Cure
The Billionaire's Secret Shoes
The Billionaire's Blizzard
The Billionaire's Chauffeuress
The Billionaire's Christmas

Want the inside scoop?
Visit robinmerrill.com to join
Robin's Readers!

Made in the USA
Columbia, SC
29 August 2020